SPOOK HOUSE

Other Avon Camelot Books by
Don Whittington

VAMPIRE MOM
WEREWOLF TONIGHT

SPOOK HOUSE

DON WHITTINGTON

AN AVON CAMELOT BOOK

SPOOK HOUSE is an original publication of Avon Books. This work has never before appeared in book form.

AVON BOOKS
A division of
The Hearst Corporation
1350 Avenue of the Americas
New York, New York 10019

Copyright © 1995 by Don Whittington
Published by arrangement with the author
Library of Congress Catalog Card Number: 95-90105
ISBN: 0-380-77937-4
RL: 4.9

First Avon Camelot Printing: October 1995

CAMELOT TRADEMARK REG. U.S. PAT. OFF. AND IN OTHER COUNTRIES, MARCA REGIS-TRADA, HECHO EN U.S.A.

Printed in the U.S.A.

OPM   10   9   8   7   6   5   4   3   2

For Emma,
my tiny dancer

Author's Note

To My Students:

Following is the third of the Chronicler's tales in the Forging of the Key. It suffers somewhat from the fact that it is a tale in which I do not appear, but compensates for this with the introduction of the first members of the New Tribe.

Further, we get our first forewarning of the epic battle which is yet so many tales away. And as always there are clues to the riddle behind the Forging of the Key. Can you find them all? If you had been the Chronicler, do you think you would have guessed your destiny? I wonder. . . .

Remember that despite their growing abilities, Winston and Broccoli are—as yet—only young boys. Sometimes they make mistakes. Big mistakes. But they never stop trying to do the right thing.

Nor should you.

So enjoy this tale of ghosts and monsters and things that go bump in the walls for its own sake. But pay attention. You never know. Later there may be a test.

—the Sage

1

"**W**ell, there it is," said Broccoli. "The Caliban House. What do you think, Winston?"

"I think we're nuts to spend the night here, that's what I think. This has nothing to do with the forging of the Key. We're just asking for trouble."

Broccoli gave me a hurt look as he shifted the camping gear on his back. "Aww, come on. It's just a haunted house. After demons and werewolves and vampires a ghost ought to be a piece of cake."

"Tell that to Booker," I said, staring up at the house.

It sat at the top of Marsten Hill overlooking our town. Once it had been a mansion, a showplace, but that had been more years ago than anyone in town could remember. Now it was just an eyesore. Its ancient wood had long since gone gray from weather, and the thick plywood that boarded the windows had buckled and split.

The front yard was a crowded riot of brambles and weeds. Vines struggled to creep up the walls, but seemed to fall away after a few feet, as if the house itself were incompatible with anything living.

The front hulked two stories tall, with sharp pitched gables that jutted at odd angles. The building swelled wider at the back and sides, so that the old structure looked like some giant toad, crouched and waiting to pounce down the hill and devour the town.

Broccoli clapped me on the shoulder. "You forget, if it wasn't for Booker we wouldn't be doing this. We can help. We may be the only ones who can. How would you feel if we did nothing and what happened to Booker happened to someone else?"

"And how will you feel," I said, "if it happens to us?" He smirked as if the very idea of a ghost getting the better of Broccoli Poe were nonsense. I sighed deeply. "Oh, never mind. You're too stubborn to listen to common sense, anyway."

There was no point arguing with Broccoli about things like this. He lived for the spooky. It was his only passion. And for some reason it had been decided that I would be his partner. Broccoli is the Key and I am the Chronicler. That meant a lot of different things, some of them pretty cool. But for now it meant that Broccoli and I were going to spend the night in the Caliban House whether I liked it or not.

The last person to do that had been Booker. Whether he'd lasted the whole night no one knew, because the next day he was found wandering the streets, his hair turned from jet black to snow white. No one knew what happened to him. He couldn't speak because his mind was gone!

That had been more than a month ago. And now we were going to see if we could learn the mystery of the Caliban House. It was true that we were likely to be a lot harder to scare than Booker had been. Battles with sorcerers and demons will do that for you. And Booker had been alone, while Broccoli and I had each other for support.

Still, faced with the looming presence of that house I regretted caving in to Broccoli's plan.

I said, "You realize that if we get stuck in there, no one's going to know where to look for us."

Broccoli shrugged. "You think if you told your dad he'd have let us come?"

"We could have told Ben."

Broccoli shook his head. "No, because he'd have insisted he come with us. Or he'd have made us bring Claude. Who knows how ghosts might react with Claude around?"

Ben was Ben Franklin—yes, *that* Ben Franklin—who lived with Broccoli as his uncle in the house next door to mine. Claude was the vampire who lived in Broccoli's basement. You think *you* have weird parents.

3

Broccoli started up the path toward the house and I trudged slowly behind him. The closer we got the more I doubted the wisdom of this adventure. The air around the place seemed thicker somehow, foul. My insides tingled with a feeling of fear and menace. I gritted my teeth and tried to shake off the feeling. "You're just nervous," I mumbled to myself.

"What?" Broccoli asked, and I just shook my head. He stopped at the NO TRESPASSING sign the city had put up by the front gate. Another sign reading, DANGER: CONDEMNED PROPERTY was nailed to the front door. "Is that new?" Broccoli asked.

I frowned. "I don't think so. This place has been condemned for as long as I've been around, anyway. I've heard my mom say it was condemned when she was a little girl. I notice nobody ever gets around to tearing it down, though."

Broccoli wrinkled his forehead in thought. His head swung from side to side as he surveyed the place. "There's definitely a presence here. Can you feel it?"

"What, are you kidding? My knees are knocking and I can barely breathe. If I felt it any more I'd need another set of drawers. Let's go home, before it's too late."

Broccoli just shook his head. "Look, I already told you. Ghosts are just unhappy spirits. If we can find out what's wrong we can help the spirit move on."

4

"Ghosts aren't the only things unhappy around this place. Certain pals of yours—namely me—are plenty unhappy, too. How come you're not helping *me* move on, huh?"

"Aww, quit your griping. You love this stuff just as much as I do." Broccoli mounted the front steps and put his hand on the doorknob. He turned to look at me. "Well? Are you coming? Or are you just chicken?" He turned and walked inside.

"Chicken, huh? I'll show you who's chicken. Where would you be if not for me, eh? You'd be wizard bait in some castle in France, that's where." I continued arguing as the door seemed to shut in my face, all by itself. "Broccoli?" I fumbled with the knob, but it wouldn't turn.

I pounded frantically on the door. "Broccoli! Are you all right? Say something, for crying out loud. BROCCOLI!"

The door opened and a smirking Broccoli Poe looked out at me. "Gotcha," he said.

Relief and anger flooded me all at once as I stared at my despicable friend. Broccoli seemed unfazed; he stared at me without blinking, his round face as serious as a car wreck.

"I guess you think that's funny," I said.

"Yes, I thought it was funny."

"How about my boot in your behind? Would that be funny?"

"Oooh, I'm all trembly. Now are you coming in, or do I have to send the ghost out to get you?"

I took a deep breath. "I'm coming," I said, and followed him in. "Jerk," I mumbled, but Broccoli only laughed as he shut the door behind us and we were enveloped by the house.

2

Oddly enough, the atmosphere wasn't quite so bad inside the house. The air was thick with mustiness and mildew, but the aura of menace I'd felt so strongly outside seemed to melt away once we entered. Despite the boarded windows enough light leaked through holes in the wall and the upper floors to see.

We found ourselves in a large room with a cold, tiled floor. A staircase beckoned to our right and doorways ran in three directions. The ceiling of this particular entrance hall ran all the way to the second floor and we could see doors hanging open above us.

The walls were stained and decaying. A fine film of plaster dust coated the floor and Broccoli and I examined the wild scuffle of footprints that must have been left by Booker in his madness.

We walked off to the left and found ourselves in

some kind of sitting room. A massive fireplace fronted one wall. You could have roasted a whole buffalo in that thing and still had room for a goat and a pot of beans. There was no furniture, except for a very old upright piano on the west wall. I plunked a key idly as Broccoli walked around the room with his arms spread wide, his eyes closed. The piano gave a halfhearted plink that did little more than irritate the spiders inside it.

"What are you doing?" I asked Broccoli.

"Looking for cold spots," he said. "In most known cases of hauntings investigators have found cold spots throughout the houses. If there's going to be a physical appearance by a ghost, a cold spot is the most likely place."

"Oh, goody," I said. I shucked my camping gear from my back and began to lay it out. Aside from our sleeping bags and flashlights we'd brought a camping lantern, a cooking ring for hot chocolate, and enough sandwiches to feed us and every ghost within three miles. My folks thought we were camping out at Forest Park.

Broccoli sighed as he finished his search for cold spots. He shrugged off his backpack and we made a little store of our things in one corner of the room.

"We've got about five hours of daylight left," he said. "I say we take the opportunity to explore the house. Who knows what we might find? Once it's dark it would be easy to get lost.''

''Sounds like a plan to me,'' I said. ''But first, let's make a pact. We stay together. None of that silly movie junk where the one guy goes by himself to investigate a noise, okay?''

Broccoli grinned. ''What's the matter? You think I'll say, 'Gee, wonder what that growling noise coming from the cellar is? Think I'll go check it out.' Give me some credit.''

''Never mind. I know you. You think you're immortal or something. Just remember to stick together.''

''Okay, I promise,'' he said. He hefted a flashlight and I grabbed mine. We'd brought extra batteries just in case. He clicked his on experimentally, then switched it off. ''We can't count on all these rooms having holes in the walls. Some are going to be pretty dark, even in the daytime.''

''Lead the way,'' I said, motioning Broccoli ahead. I followed him back to the big room we'd first entered, then left down a dank hallway. The odor of rotting wallpaper tickled my nose.

The first room was to our left, behind the room with the fireplace. It was long and four tall windows ran the length of it. A door in back led somewhere. Again there was no furniture. An ancient chandelier, thick with cobwebs, hung from the ceiling.

"Dining room, I'll bet. That door probably goes to the kitchen or some kind of serving area," Broccoli said. I followed him there, and we walked through into a strange room lined with shelves on either side.

"I know what this is," I said. "It's probably where they stored the china and stuff like that. My Aunt Brenda has a room like this in her house."

Beyond the china space lay the kitchen. Unlike the other rooms we'd seen, this one was almost furnished. A large wood stove stood leaning against one wall. Its rear legs had broken off leaving it tilted. A smallish wooden box sat next to a large wooden cupboard. I opened the box and peered inside.

"That's an icebox," Broccoli said. "See, they'd put a big block of ice up top here, and then keep milk and cheese and stuff in the bottom."

"Geez, nobody's lived in this place since electricity."

"They had gas though. See those old fixtures on the wall? Those are gas jets, for lamps."

The gas jets were simple juts of pipe that crooked upward. A valve was set in the wall by each lamp. You could tell that once there had been some kind of glass bowl that had sat in the fixture.

A large, free-standing cast-iron sink stood against the far wall. The rear windows were only partially boarded and quite a bit of light came through. I peeked through a window to see the overgrown back-yard. Several iron benches were scattered around back there. A crumbling stone wall rose about a hundred feet away and ran in curious curves up the hillside. There were a couple of humps of something along the wall, but they were so covered with vines I couldn't make them out.

We spent the next hour searching the other rooms, but all were empty. One was apparently a library or study, since its walls were lined with bookshelves, and another smaller fireplace was set against the outer wall. The other rooms gave no clues to their purposes, although we made guesses about sewing rooms, music rooms, and bedrooms. A storage cellar lay below the kitchen, and there were still some old jars and things in there.

Fact is, there just wasn't much in the way of spooky stuff to report. Broccoli checked for cold spots in every room and found none. We felt no bad vibrations anywhere. We found little sign of anyone who'd ever lived there. It was the most boring haunted house I'd ever heard of.

Disgusted, we decided to check the backyard. We were looking for a basement, something separate from the cellar, like so many old houses had back in those days. Instead, Broccoli was attracted by the strange old wall and we went over there to investigate.

The humps I'd seen turned out to be statues. Broccoli and I grunted as we started stripping vines from them. There were two, set several yards apart. The statues were of a man and a woman. I can no more describe the woman's unearthly beauty than I can explain the desperate weariness and torment of the man. Yet these things were obvious to us just by looking at them. The artist had been a person of rare skill to capture such qualities.

"How could something like this still be here, untouched after all these years?" I asked.

Broccoli shook his head, wonderingly. "I have no idea. That man looks so—so tortured! And she— could there ever have been a woman so beautiful?"

I pulled away more weeds near the base of her statue.

"There's some kind of inscription plate," I said. Once cleared, the plate was still hard to read, as the years had taken a toll on the chiseled lettering. We could barely make out a woman's name. MADELINE.

Broccoli scrabbled at the other statue, but I just stared at the name before me. One of the things that happens to me as the Chronicler is that I get these flashes of insight, of truth. It was happening to me now, and the dread I had felt before was replaced by a kind of expectant tingle.

Broccoli said, "It's clearer than the other one. It says—"

"I know what it says," I interrupted. I gave Broccoli a curious smile. "It says, RODERICK."

"Huh? How do you know?" Broccoli asked, astonished.

I stood and looked back at the house. "I have no idea," I said. "But I think we're going to find out"—a cold breeze suddenly made me shudder—"tonight!"

3

We reentered the house through the kitchen door. We were on our way back to where we'd left our stuff when Broccoli put a hand on my arm, stopping me.

"Look," he said.

He was pointing at the icebox, and at first I didn't understand. Then I saw the slight trickle of dampness seeping from the bottom of the door.

"What the . . . ?" I opened the icebox, and it was jammed full. A porcelain pitcher with light blue flowers painted on the side bulged on the bottom shelf amid waxed paper bundles. A slightly melting block of ice sat above. I pulled out the drain pan below the ice and found it half full.

I raised my eyebrows as I looked at Broccoli. "This was *not* here a minute ago."

Broccoli grabbed one of the bundles and unwrapped it. A yellow-white, shapeless mound was inside. He sniffed it curiously, then pinched off a bit and tasted it. "It's butter," he said thoughtfully. He rewrapped it and pulled out another bundle.

"You sure you should eat that?" I asked doubtfully.

"Why not? Seems solid enough. Look, this one's some kind of cheese." Broccoli wrinkled his nose in disgust. "Pyew! How can anybody eat this junk?" He shoved it back in the icebox and closed the door.

"Look around," he said. "See if anything else has changed."

I started opening cupboards, but found nothing. I went to the large wooden chest and opened the door. "There's a half-eaten pie here," I said.

"Really?" Broccoli peered with interest over my shoulder. "I wondered what this thing was. Must be what they called a pie safe."

"Who cares what they called it, man? Where'd this stuff come from?" I looked around nervously and noticed the gas jet on the wall. "Like that. I know that fixture wasn't there before." A delicate, tulip-shaped piece of glass now sat on the jet. I could almost imagine a flame sputtering inside it. The second fixture remained bare.

"Come on," said Broccoli. "Let's see if there's anything else."

We crept through the little china closet to the dining room. The dining room had changed. A faded tapestry now hung on the wall across from the win-

15

dows, and a huge piece of wooden furniture, a sideboard, ran the length of the back wall.

"Now, somebody might have added that stuff in the kitchen as some kind of joke," I whispered, "but nobody could have moved that hulking piece of wood in here without us hearing them. Besides, we couldn't have been outside more than twenty minutes."

Broccoli closed his eyes and held his hands out as if trying to feel the air around him. He stopped and looked back at me, frustrated.

"I don't understand this at all. Obviously something really weird is going on. This house is somehow—I don't know how to say it—I guess, reanimating itself. I should be able to sense some kind of spiritual energy but there's nothing. Outside I was sure I felt something, but in here—zip."

I didn't feel good about this at all. Broccoli was like a Geiger counter for occult stuff. If I couldn't count on his peculiar talents, I didn't care much for my chances.

"Look, there's still lots of daylight left. What say we get our stuff and book it out of here? Whatever we expected, this isn't it. We can consult with our spirit guide. Maybe she can tell us something about this place."

Broccoli threw me a stubborn look. "I wish you'd stop complaining. This is a lot more interesting than it is scary. I say we stick it out. *I* came here to spend the night, and darn it, that's what I'm going to do. With you or without you."

"Oh yeah? I'll bet you wouldn't stay five minutes in this place without me to back you up."

"Says who?"

"Says me."

"Okay. Bet," he said, and I could tell from his eyes he meant it. For about the hundredth time since I'd met him I kicked myself mentally for letting him pull me into these stupid schemes.

"Oh, all right. So you're brave as a lion. Big deal. I still say this is stupid."

"So leave," he said calmly.

"Nah, I can't leave. You'd do something hammer-headed, and I'd have to bail you out again."

"Yeah, right," he said, but I knew he was secretly relieved. Like I said, we're a team.

He put a hand on my shoulder. "Let's go back to the room where we left our gear, just in case some way heavy piece of furniture is sitting on it now."

"Yeah, okay." I jerked away from his hand so he'd know I was still teed off at him. Just because he'd won the argument didn't mean I had to act as if I liked it. I figured I could sulk for a good hour at least.

My attitude bothered him, and I knew it, which is why I enjoyed it so much. He couldn't help himself. He was still trying to cheer me up.

"You'll see," he was saying, "this is going to be fun."

I stepped through the door to the sitting room and I was grabbed suddenly in a grip of steel. A muscular arm was across my throat squeezing the breath from me.

"All right, you," said a voice. "Who are you and what do you think you're doing here?" Behind me I could hear Broccoli wrestling on the floor with someone else.

All I could think of at the time was that it was so unfair. The ghosts were attacking us, and it wasn't even dark yet.

Then the grip on my throat tightened, and I passed out.

4

Someone was arguing as I came to.

"What did you think you were doing? You could have killed him."

"Aww, come on, Encarna. I didn't mean to hurt him."

I fluttered my eyes and looked into the soft, brown face of an angel. She looked worried staring down at me. My head rested in her lap, and she patted my cheek gently.

"Are you okay, little guy?" she asked.

My throat still hurt. I rasped, "I—I think so. Who are you?"

"I'm Encarna. Encarna Velasquez. I'm sorry this lummox hurt you, but you scared us."

I sat up slowly, reluctant to move away from this beautiful girl. Broccoli sat between two guys I didn't know.

He said, "That is no excuse for jumping us like

19

that." He looked at the guy to his right, a thin boy not much taller than Broccoli with thick glasses and unruly red hair. He frowned at Broccoli, and didn't look all that apologetic.

The lummox was a lot bigger than either Broccoli or me. He wore a muscle shirt to show off his powerful arms and chest. He hung his head sheepishly under Encarna's glare.

"Aww, heck. I already apologized."

I felt gingerly at my throat. "I'm okay," I said, my voice stronger now. "But who are you people?"

The big guy shot me a hard glance. "I think we should be asking the questions here."

"Be quiet, Deion. He's just a little kid."

I sat up straighter, offended. "And who are you, Grandma? You can't be more than fourteen."

"Fifteen," she answered. She smiled crookedly. "And how old are you, Grandpa? Eleven?"

"Twelve. Almost thirteen." I glared over at Deion, acting like I didn't care how big and tough he was. Yeah, right.

"Kids," he said, disgusted. "Do your folks know you're playing over here?"

"No. Do yours?" I shot back.

Deion swelled a little, and I thought he was going to reach over and thump me.

Broccoli put a hand on the black kid's arm. "Just settle down. We've had enough fighting. Look, I don't think that you guys ought to be here. This place is dangerous, and I don't know if Winston and I can protect you.''

The three older kids looked at Broccoli in astonishment. They couldn't believe this chubby little kid would talk about protecting *them*. Meanwhile Broccoli just returned their stares.

The kid with the glasses turned to me. ''Is he putting us on?''

I smiled. ''He's as serious as cancer.'' As I looked at the boy's face I had another flash of insight. He was the most tense of the group, and I could almost feel waves of guilt and fear coming from him.

Encarna had said something I didn't catch, and Broccoli was shaking his head. ''I'm sorry you think we're just fooling around, but we're not. What I don't understand is why you three are here?''

''None of your business,'' said Deion.

''Oh, put a sock in it,'' I said. ''They're here because they feel responsible for what happened to Booker. They think it's their fault.''

Now it was my turn to be stared at in astonishment. Encarna trembled slightly, and put a shaky hand out to touch Deion. ''How? How do you know . . . ?''

Broccoli rose and walked over to his backpack. ''He just knows,'' he said, then rummaged in his pack for a candy bar. He sighed as he unwrapped the bar and took a bite. He looked out at the entrance area,

21

then looked over at me. "More furniture," he said, and walked out of the room.

"What does that mean? More furniture?" asked the guy with the glasses.

"The house appears to be adding things. Changing as the day wears on. When we came in the place was empty. Now there's furniture. It's like the place is . . ."

"Coming back to life," Encarna finished for me. She stood and reached out for the wall. She held her hand flat against the dingy wallpaper. "It's like I told you. The house isn't haunted." She turned to look at us, her eyes glowing. "It's alive!"

I turned that over in my mind for a second. It didn't strike me as quite true, but I decided against saying anything.

Deion's expression was openly skeptical, and the other guy just looked miserable.

Encarna came to me and squatted beside me. "What do you know about all this? Why are you here?"

Deion said, "Give it a rest, woman. They're just snot-nosed kids who think they're on some kind of stupid adventure. It's bad enough we have to be here. Pete," he said, finally giving me a name for the boy in glasses, "gather up their gear. I'm throwing them out before they really do get hurt."

Broccoli stood leaning against the doorjamb. "Lots

22

of luck," he said. "I just tried all the doors. They won't open." He looked at his nails, and I grinned to myself realizing he was showing off. He looked up again. "So I suspect we should share what we know while we can. Because none of us are leaving here until we solve the mystery of this house. Or until it lets us leave."

"What if . . . what if it doesn't let us leave?" Pete asked in a quiet whisper.

Broccoli shrugged. "Why wouldn't it? It let Booker leave. When it was done with him."

"Oh geez," Pete wailed and covered his face with his hands. "I *knew* this was a bad idea. I knew it, I knew it, I knew it."

Deion rushed from the room, and in seconds I heard him pounding frantically against the door and cursing with rage. Encarna sat looking miserable, her back against the wall, her eyes looking at the clenched fists in her lap.

Deion burst back into the room, his breath coming in gasps, his eyes wide.

"He's not lying. I can't even batter through them."

Pete groaned loudly as Encarna whispered to herself, "What have we done? Great Spirit, what have we done?"

Deion walked angrily back and forth like a caged tiger. Suddenly he stopped, head cocked, listening.

"What's that?" he asked.

The sound started softly then rose, spiraling through the air like a tornado. Mad, cackling laughter seemed to come from all around us. Deion crouched in a corner, his gaze shooting everywhere like a man who expects attack from all directions. Pete lay huddled on the floor, his hands over his ears.

Then it was over, and the silence seemed nearly as loud as the laughter had been. I crawled to Pete on my hands and knees and put my face close to his.

"Boo!" I shouted, and he almost screamed.

I rose and sneered at Broccoli. "And they think we're the ones who should have left. Criminey, what a bunch of wimps!"

It got to them. Deion said something really nasty to me, but I let it pass. I knew what it felt like to be that scared, and I wasn't unsympathetic. But Broccoli and I had been through a lot. And laughter—mad and ghostly as it may be—was only noise, after all. If I was right we'd all be in for a lot worse before the night was over.

Broccoli started setting up the gas ring. Pete was standing now with Encarna and Deion. The three of them were trying to silently comfort each other without actually looking at each other.

"They'll be all right," Broccoli whispered to me as he worked. I nodded.

"What are you doing?" asked Encarna.

24

"Making cocoa," Broccoli said. "It's the cure for everything. Ghosts, ghouls, and goblins all lose their power before a nice cup of hot chocolate."

She giggled, and I knew that—for now at least—they were going to be okay. I got a package of paper cups and passed them around. I got to Deion and he stopped me.

"You weren't frightened at all, were you? Why not? Who are you kids?"

"We're, uh—well, that's a long story. Maybe we'll share it with you later. If we all survive, that is. In the meantime, you'd better tell us what brought the three of you together. It might be important, and it will help pass the time until ..." I stopped myself and went back to get my chocolate.

"Until what?" asked Pete. "What were you going to say?"

"It doesn't matter."

"No," said Encarna. "Finish. We're all in this together."

I sighed deeply and shared a knowing glance with Broccoli.

"Until the house decides what it's going to do with us," he answered for me.

The room had grown steadily darker as we talked, so I lit the camping lantern. Broccoli looked at his watch.

"What time is it?" I asked.

25

"Too early to be dark. I suspect that time has been distorted in here somehow."

"Something's up," said Deion softly. He peered through a split in the boarded window. "It's nighttime out there."

We gathered in a little circle on the floor, sipping our hot drink and taking comfort in the glow from the lantern.

"Well? You want to tell us your story?" Broccoli asked.

Encarna started to speak, then stopped, looking upward. Broccoli put his hand in hers and gave it a reassuring squeeze.

"Just ignore it. Tell us what happened."

Haltingly, Encarna began to speak.

And in the rooms above we heard things moving.

5

"**P**ete, why don't you tell it. It's really your story."
Pete nodded and pushed his glasses up his nose.

"It all starts with Booker. He's been sort of my special torment since first grade. Dad always says that bullies are really cowards, and that if you just stand up to them once, they will leave you alone. He's always saying things like that, and it makes me wonder, sometimes, how many other lies he's been telling me.

"Seems to me kids become bullies because they are bigger and tougher than anybody else their age. Like Deion, except he's not a bully."

"You could have fooled me," I muttered.

"Aww, he's just nervous. He didn't mean it. Not like Booker. Anyway, things have been better for me with Booker the last year or so. Junior High is a lot bigger than grade school. It's easier to lose yourself. And once Deion and I became friends, well, Booker doesn't want to mess with Deion."

Pete looked at his friend with an embarrassed smile, and I noticed for the first time that Deion seemed genuinely fond of this gawky, brainy boy.

"But nothing lasts forever. It was at PE during a soccer game. Booker was on our team, and I let one get away from me. He just exploded, and before I could react he was hitting me, knocking me down, kicking me.

"The coach wasn't there, of course. They never are when something like that happens. It's like a law of nature or something. But Deion was, and he pulled Booker off me. That's when all the girls came over from the other field to watch."

Pete looked at Encarna. "Now it's your turn to tell what happened."

Encarna sighed. "It just made me mad. Two grown boys, men almost, threatening each other like some kind of animals. I'd seen that Booker before. I knew what kind of jerk he was. So I hit him where he lives. I called him a coward."

She sipped at her chocolate as we waited. The noises upstairs were muffled, but they were still there. From time to time Deion looked up at the ceiling, frowning. It sounded like someone heavy walking.

"It got to be a shouting match, with me calling him a chicken and him saying he wasn't and then— I don't know why, really—I just said, prove it. And I dared him to spend the night here. Alone." She

28

wiped a tear from her cheek. "And the dumb jerk agreed." She turned from Broccoli to me and back again. "So you see, it's all my fault. I dared him, and now his spirit is captured in this house. All because of me."

Deion spoke. "Stop that, Encarna. We were all part of it. We met him here. We made sure he followed through. We watched him go inside."

"That's right," said Pete. "And we're back, too. Maybe it took us a month to work up our nerve, but we're back, and we're going to make it right."

Pete's voice was a little shaky, but there was nothing weak about his eyes. I saw grim determination there, and revised my opinion of Pete upward. He may have been frail, but he would do.

The noise from upstairs had grown quiet, and we grew quiet as well, each lost in his own thoughts.

At last Broccoli said, "What did you mean about Booker's spirit being trapped in this house?"

Encarna gave him a guilty look. "I guess I should admit I know more about this house than most people do. My Great-Grandmother worked here, many years ago. I learned from her that the house is alive, evil. It's like a huge battery powered by the souls of those it captures."

"Your Great-Grandmother told you this?"

"Yes. She—how do I say this?—she's a spirit walker."

Broccoli gave her a surprised look. "Really?"

Encarna nodded and I said, "I don't understand. What does that mean?"

"It means she's dead, Winston. And you speak with her often?" Broccoli asked her.

"Only when I need guidance. It is foolish to speak with the dead without purpose."

Broccoli almost beamed. "You speak with other dead, too? That means you're a shaman. Hot dog! I've always wanted to learn about Native American magic."

"You never told us that before," said Deion quietly.

"It's not the sort of thing that comes up a lot. I didn't want you to think I was strange," she said.

It fell quiet again and there was nothing to do but think. Shadows cast by our lantern loomed on the walls around us. I thought for a moment the shadows were moving by themselves, but as soon as I really looked they seemed to stop. I shivered a little despite my bluff of bravery.

"Well, we can't sit here all night," Broccoli said.

I snorted. "Why not? Make the spooks come to us, that's what I say."

"I'm with him," said Pete.

Broccoli shook his head. "Look, if she's right, if this house is collecting souls, then that means there is some kind of charm here, a physical device like a sculpture or a talisman that is central to its power. If we can find it, perhaps we can remove whatever kind of sorcery powers it."

"I thought we were looking for ghosts," I said.

"We are. But even in ordinary hauntings a ghost is tied to something, a room, or a house, or perhaps a spot of land. If there are many ghosts here, then probably something attracts them. Something cursed."

"What kind of kid talks about 'ordinary hauntings'?" asked Pete.

Encarna rubbed fretfully at her forehead. "Hey, what gives? What is that?" She wiped again. "There it goes again. Is something leaking?"

Deion lifted the lantern, held it close to Encarna's face. Her forehead was smeared with blood.

"Oh, geez," whispered Pete.

Broccoli shined his flashlight toward the ceiling. "It's coming from up there," he said thoughtfully.

Blood hung and dripped from a dark stain in the ceiling above Encarna's head. She scrambled away from the drip in disgust.

"Can ghosts bleed real blood?" I asked.

Broccoli stood and wagged the beam of his flashlight toward the door. "Let's go find out."

31

6

We stepped into the cold entryway, and I now saw ta-
bles against the wall. They held delicate vases with black-
ened, rotting flowers. Mirrors hung on two walls, and I
turned my eyes for fear of what I might see in them.

We moved up the staircase in a tight clump. Everyone but Broccoli seemed nervous, and it irritated me
that he took all this so casually. I wasn't scared exactly—well, not much anyway—but the closer we got
to the top of the stairs the more I convinced myself
I wasn't going to like what I found.

"This is the door," Broccoli whispered as he
turned the knob. All of us played our flashlights
through the doorway.

"There's nothing there," said Deion.

"No, look," said Pete, pointing. A puddle of blood
lay spread across the floor like a rug. It was hard to
see until the light hit it just right, and then you wondered how you could have ever missed it.

"It's an illusion. It has to be," said Deion, stepping through the door. Broccoli followed him, and then the rest of us trailed behind.

"Why did we have to come in here?" I asked. "So now we know what's dripping. Big deal. Let's go."

"It's not very scary is it?" said Deion. "I mean it's weird enough but . . ."

"Look," said Broccoli quietly.

The puddle began to roil and move, and Deion backed away from it. A clump of something formed in the center. The door behind us slammed shut by itself.

"Oh, geez," whined Pete.

The pool swirled violently now, curling, clotting, shuddering into some vaguely human shape. A low moan escaped from the creature, and I felt pure unreasoning terror at the sound.

When the figure turned at last we could see it was an old woman, a hag. Her wrinkled face was covered with splotches.

She opened her mouth and a harsh, rasping sound came out.

"You will die here," she said, and her lips twisted in a snarl.

"Who are you?" asked Encarna.

The crone tilted her head and regarded the girl. "You have no power here, shaman."

Encarna lifted her head proudly. No fear showed

33

in her face. "I am a speaker to the dead. You have no choice but to answer me, spirit."

The hag ambled toward Encarna who, despite herself, stepped backward.

"And what . . ."—she moved closer—". . . makes you think . . ."—she reached with a clawed hand—". . . I'm dead, my sweet?" She grabbed Encarna by the shoulder and pulled her to her. The hag opened her mouth and in the flashlight's glare I saw rows of needle teeth. Before she could move, Broccoli leaped onto her back.

Immediately the hag screamed, and we cringed at the pure, unholy rage in that sound. Smoke rose from her body where Broccoli touched her. She staggered back away from him in agony.

"The robe," she moaned. "He has the robe." Other voices began to reverberate around the room as if dozens of spirits were there with us all babbling excitedly.

"The robe."

"He has the robe."

"The master will have him now."

"The robe of miracles."

"He is doomed . . . he is doomed . . . he is doomed."

Deion threw himself at the door and dragged it open slowly as if something powerful were holding on the other side. We clambered through to get away from the crone and her voices.

On the landing wisps of mist were swirling at the head of the stairs. The vague outline of a man in a cape appeared. It swept upon us in a heartbeat. The mist enveloped Broccoli, its colors flashing like a light show. We heard more whispering voices.

"It is true. The robe is here. He has the robe."

And with that the ghost disappeared into thin air. Broccoli stood shivering.

"So cold. I wouldn't have thought anything could be that cold!"

I put my arms around him and led him back down the stairs. We adjourned to what we had come to think of as our room.

"Are you all right?" Deion was asking Encarna.

"Thanks to him. What was that thing? It was going to kill me."

"Yeah," I said, and poked Broccoli who was wrapping himself in a sleeping bag. "Whatever happened to your old 'Ghosts can't hurt you' theory, eh?"

He glared at me. "So I was wrong. So sue me."

Pete hunkered down next to Broccoli. "You getting any warmer?"

"Yes, thank goodness. I don't ever want to feel that cold again."

"Good. Now what exactly is going on? What is all this business about a robe?"

"The Robe of the Thaumaturge," I said.

Pete looked at me. "Thaumaturge, huh? That means miracle worker. The 'robe of miracles,' something said upstairs. Sounds handy. Where is it?"

I pointed at Broccoli. "Inside him. He absorbed it when we went to . . . never mind. Anyway, that's what they mean. He has other stuff in him, too, but the robe seems to have really turned on whatever's controlling this house."

Broccoli blinked as everybody stared at him. "Well don't look at me. I just absorbed it. I can't use it. I don't know how."

"But I do," said a voice. A dark figure stood at the doorway. A long cape hung from his shoulders. Beside him stood a slavering hound, a huge ugly dog that growled menacingly. The figure looked down at the animal.

"Kill everyone except the fat one. Leave him for me."

And the dog leaped for Pete's neck.

7

Now you may remember a while back that I said Broccoli was the Key and I was the Chronicler. I told you then some of what it meant to be the Chronicler, but not all.

Apparently, whatever power had decided to link Broccoli and me together had also decided that I was going to be the muscle more often than not to protect the Key. Nobody had consulted me about it, so I was pretty much stuck with the job.

But one of the things I had gained along the way was a sword. A magic sword, that stayed hidden in some other dimension unless I desperately needed it. As the hound leaped at Pete the sword appeared magically in my hand.

Now, you should understand that I am not a tough kid. I never took any martial arts, and the few times I ever got in a scuffle at school I was whipped more often than I came out ahead. But when that sword is in my hand I am not Winston anymore, but the Chronicler, a creature of power.

And I can move like lightning.

I slammed the dog away from Pete with the side of the blade. Behind me I heard Deion going, "What the . . . ?" but I kept my attention focused on the hound. It cringed against the wall growling at me, looking for an opening. My sword kept it well at bay.

The figure in the doorway spoke. "Fool, do you think you can kill this hound?" The cape covered the figure's entire form, and a trick of lighting hid its face. Only a pair of red shining eyes shone from its cowled head.

I felt my mouth stretch in a wicked, warrior's grin. "Mister, I can just about guarantee it. First it," I waggled the sword at the dog, then at the figure, "then you."

The eyes of the figure glowed brighter. "Do not mock me, child."

"Wouldn't dream of it."

The dog, unable to get at me, had grabbed my backpack, and was tearing at it savagely. The figure waved his hand and the dog, along with my backpack and all my food, vanished into nothingness against the wall. I straightened and gave the figure my full attention.

"Very well," it said. "The night is long, and I have time. And you are arrogant. We of the skull have seen much, we have battled much, and we thrive. Can you say as much, young warrior?''

I grinned. ''We have stood on the plains of Evil, and returned of our own will and power. Can you say as much? Or did you think we picked up the Robe of the Thaumaturge at the local Wal-Mart?''

The figure chuckled. ''Oh my, yes, you are arrogant. It will prove your undoing. We will come in force next time.'' He began to vanish, wisping away like smoke. ''Wait for us . . . wait for us.'' And he was gone.

I turned to see the others staring at me. I lifted my sword arm and smiled as my trusty friend vanished to whatever world it keeps itself. I grinned self-consciously.

Pete licked his lips. ''Who *are* you guys?''

I looked at Broccoli for advice, but he just shrugged. ''You're the Chronicler. You tell them.''

I sighed, and sat on the floor. Slowly the others sat as well.

''Go on,'' said Encarna.

''Well, it all started with the Amber Man,'' I said, and then told the stories which have come to be called *Werewolf Tonight* and *Vampire Mom* by the folklorists. When I'd finished everyone sat quietly sort of taking it all in.

The house had settled into deep quiet as I spoke, and I had the nervous feeling it had listened as well.

Deion nudged Pete's arm and said, "What do you think, Pete? You're into all this fantasy stuff. Are these guys on the level or are they playing some weird version of Dungeons and Dragons?"

Pete blinked thoughtfully and wiped his glasses on the tail of his shirt. He said, "It's kind of hard to doubt a guy who can summon a magic sword. And we all heard the ghosts talking about the robe. No, I'm sure these two are what they say they are. What I don't know is what it means."

I heard a sudden intake of breath, and turned to see Encarna staring at the doorway.

"That man," she said. "He looks so sad."

We all turned to see a thin, pale figure standing in the door. He watched us with mournful eyes. He looked behind him as if frightened of something, then turned back to us, his finger to his lips, motioning us to silence.

He tried to move inside the room with us, but his movements were jerky, as if some force were working against him. Despite the effort he managed to work his way along the wall to the great fireplace. His face strained with effort as he reached a trembling hand and pointed to something at the hearth.

"What is he doing?" asked Pete. "What's wrong with him?"

His form shook crazily, and bits of him began to tear away like strips of crepe paper that floated above us and out of the room. With great effort he pointed one last time at the hearth, then surrendered to whatever force was fighting him, and swirled in pieces over our heads to vanish floating in the entry hall.

"What the heck was that all about?" said Deion.

"It's the room," said Broccoli.

"Yes," said Pete. "That's why that other creature didn't step inside here. He had to send the dog—the hell hound. This room is somehow forbidden to them."

Encarna shuddered and wrapped her arms around herself. "Thank goodness for that. Then all we have to do is stay here until morning. If they can't get to us then they can't hurt us."

Broccoli shook his head as he rose to his feet. "Hardly. That ghost managed to get in here, remember. It was hard for him, but he still managed it. This room may be an effective barrier against a ghost, but there are more than ghosts at work in this house."

He walked to the fireplace and began studying the bricks around the hearth.

Deion joined him and asked, "What are you doing?"

"That ghost went to a lot of painful trouble trying to show us something. I think we should see what we can find. See if any of these bricks are loose."

They began tugging at the bricks, and studying the wall around the hearth with their flashlights.

41

Encarna said, "I wonder who that was. He seemed different from those other two. Much sadder and—more helpless somehow."

"His name is Roderick," I said.

From the fireplace Broccoli said, "I wondered if you recognized him."

Encarna raised her eyebrows in question. I explained. "Broccoli and I found these two statues out back of a man and a woman. The names Roderick and Madeline were carved at the base of each."

"Roderick and Madeline? Are you sure?" asked Pete, suddenly excited.

I looked at him, confused by his eagerness. "Why, yes, I'm sure."

"Ahh," said Deion. "Found you, you rascal. Look at this, Broccoli."

We watched as a brick slid from the hearth, revealing a deep hole. Broccoli shone his flashlight inside and grunted.

"Huh, how 'bout that." He reached in and brought out a tattered notebook.

He and Deion returned with the notebook and rejoined our circle. Before Broccoli could even open the book Pete had snatched it from him. "Hey!" Broccoli said, but Pete ignored him.

His face lit up as he began to read the first pages then he looked at us excitedly. "Do you know what this is? I was suspicious when Winston said the names Roderick and Madeline, but this—this proves it. Listen." He began to read from the book:

"It is with no small amount of trepidation that I share these, my darkest fears, lest they be discovered by my tender host and further burden his feelings of enormous guilt. Yet I must state what I have seen to someone, if only to this dumb parchment ere I go mad myself. Indeed, my fears extend not only for my corporeal being but for my immortal soul as well, and as my hosts know me by no other name than Edgar Perry, should I die in this place not even the meagre few who love me would know to pray for my soul's deliverance. Should circumstance determine I must hide this document; then know that all has gone ill, and I ask the discoverer therefore send to my people in the east, to John Allan of Richmond, Virginia. Tell him his adopted son Edgar has died, and that in the end I forgave him everything."

Pete looked up again. We all stared at him, baffled. "Well, don't you see?" he said. "Edgar Perry. John Allan. Edgar Perry was the name he took when he fled his adopted father. John Allan pretty much disowned him when he went into the army, so he

43

took the name of Edgar Perry. But his real name is Edgar Allan Poe!''

"You're right," said Encarna. "I remember when we studied American literature. I mean, I don't remember all those details like you do, but I remember the story, that he changed his name for a while. But if this was written by Edgar Allan Poe . . . he didn't die here. He died out east somewhere.''

"Yes, I know," said Pete. "But what if he thought he had to hide this. Because he thought he was going to die. And then he managed to get away. And having got away, he was in no mood to return for it. But think. Roderick and Madeline. Don't you know where we are?''

Deion's eyes opened wider as recognition hit him. "Holy cow! I get it. I remember the story. Brother and sister weren't they? And he buried her alive.''

Broccoli frowned. "Then you're saying that we've found the house from that famous story. That the House of Caliban is really . . .''

"The House of Usher!" Pete finished for him.

8

Okay, I admit it. I was the only one in the room who had not read "The Fall of the House of Usher" by Edgar Allan Poe. Not only had I not read it, I'd never heard of it.

So sue me.

I was actually a little put out by the whole thing. Usually I was the one who figured these things out. Suddenly I was the only one who had to have things explained. I knew it was childish to feel the way I did, but I couldn't help it. I pretended not to pay too much attention to their conversation, but of course I heard everything.

"Obviously," Pete was saying, "it was always the House of Caliban, and he just changed it to Usher when he wrote the story. I wonder how closely it ties to what he actually went through when he stayed here."

Broccoli said, "Probably not much. But the best way to find out is to read the journal."

Pete started reading, and I tried to follow along. The language was very old fashioned, and used a lot of words I didn't know, so it was a little hard to follow in places. We still have the journal, of course, and I've copied some of the most pertinent parts here.

February 2, 1831

My mind is no longer master of my nights, but slinks before an army of nightmare beings, hideous gargoyles great with blood lust and evil. I, who wrote such poetry of beauty, can no longer summon an image unmarked by grotesquerie. Even awake, I dare not trust my senses. Rising from a most horrible dream last night I sought a mirror and saw staring back at me from its Plutonian depths a skull, red tinged and shaped entirely from crystal. The sockets of its eyes swirled with carmine flames and from its lips worms writhed and fluid bubbled. The worst thing of all is that despite my cries of terror no one came. No one came.

And this:

February 5, 1831

There is but one within these walls I fain to trust, and she a pagan Indian such as those who hung outside our soldier's camps to beg for food last winter. She has that mysterious quality of judgement so common among the older Indians, a way of regarding whites as if with pity. No doubt it is that very quality which drives so many of our kind mad with slaughter to be done with them forever from our continent, as if by proving their opinion of us we might deny its truth.

"Could that have been your great grandmother?" Pete asked.

Encarna shook her head. "I don't see how. But maybe. She was very old."

And this:

February 7, 1831

How can I describe the horror that I feel. This morning as I prowled within the vaults beneath the house searching for Roderick, fearing that at last he'd taken his own frail life, I came across the lady, Madeline. Bowing, as any would on meeting their lady at such early hours, I was struck by the blackness of her feet, bare against the copper-clad flooring of the entry. Her gown was spattered with bits of filth from which an odour of decay reeked forth. She smiled like a

47

ghoul and licked some watery fluid from her hand.

She made as if to speak when suddenly Roderick appeared, rushing to take her by the arms and lead her up the broken stone stairway to the house. "Forgive her," he said, "she's not been well." And she said nothing, content to be led like a sleepy child within his arms. But as they moved away she looked back at me, and though no words passed between us I knew that she was staying now each night among the dead and in her eyes I saw an invitation that chills my soul to even dwell upon. No! No! I will say no more of this horror!

Finally, there was this:

February 9, 1831

I am convinced that doom and tragedy will soon befall, and I must escape. Strange forces— forces beyond the knowledge or authority of my hosts—conspire to keep me here, but I believe the Indian woman will help me away. I will secret this book at some safe place, and hope there is never a need for it to be found. I believe there is more to this Indian than first appears. I have seen her when she thinks I am not looking, when she is busy at her cleaning, and I have noticed how light seems to shine from her in the darkest corners of the house. It is a healthy glow, a spiritual nimbus I had long thought reserved for saints.

Yesterday she told me that the house itself is alive and powerful—no, not the house itself so much as this place on the earth. She said that there are lines of force upon the earth, lines which intersect and form loci of power which those with knowledge can exploit. She says this spot is a place of powerful medicine which was known to the Indians for centuries before the white man came.

She then took a small, blue crystal from a bag about her neck and rubbed it softly across a scar on my hand. She chanted as she did this, but I could not make out the sense of what she sang. A slight tingle danced across my skin at the touch of that cool stone. "The loci," she said to me, returning the crystal to her bag, "cares not how the power is used. It is neutral. So do not curse this place for being. That is the way of the fool. Places cannot be evil. Only people."

The refined, scientific gentleman of this modern age will no doubt laugh at such foolish lore, but when I look into this woman's eyes I remember Hamlet's warning to Horatio, and I keep counsel to myself. But I swear to you that as I write this now, I look at my hand, and the scar I carried for the last ten years has vanished!

There was a lot more than that in the notebook, but you get the main idea. Everyone sat quietly thinking about the things that Pete had read to us.

He shoved his glasses higher on his nose. "If I remember right, this would all have occurred between the time he was kicked out of West Point and before he began his literary career in earnest. From his comments in here it seems that Roderick is someone he met during his years in the regular army, before West Point."

"How do you know so much about Edgar Allan Poe?" I asked.

Pete laughed. "He's kind of a hobby of mine. I did my main composition project on him last year. Got an A."

"You always get As," Deion teased and slapped Pete on the arm.

I snorted and said, "Maybe you should be the Chronicler."

Encarna frowned at the sarcasm in my voice. "Cripes, what a baby. What's your problem, anyway?"

I didn't say anything. I moved to our stuff, and gave one longing thought to my vanished backpack.

I'd had a Butterfinger and a can of Pepsi in there that would have been just right. I started rummaging in Broccoli's stuff for something to eat.

Truth to tell I was feeling antsy. Just sitting and listening to Pete read had taken almost all of my willpower. I didn't like just sitting in that room waiting for that stupid house to fall on us. I wanted to be doing something.

On the other hand, I couldn't think of anything useful to do.

Broccoli and Pete were deep in conversation, going over clues from Poc's notes. Deion was talking quietly to Encarna. I was definitely a fifth wheel all of a sudden, and I didn't like it a bit.

There was nothing in our stuff I wanted to eat. I remembered how food had started appearing in the kitchen earlier. Broccoli had said it tasted all right, but was it safe to eat ghost food?

The more I thought of that kitchen the better I liked it. By now it might be fully stocked with red, luscious hams and three-tiered chocolate cakes. Food became the single most important thing in the world, suddenly, and I stood, determined to go get some. I looked at the others, so smug and self-important. To heck with them, let them get their own food.

I slipped quietly out of the room, hoping they didn't see me. It would be just like them to beat me there and get all the best stuff. That's just the way they were, the jerks. Never appreciated the things *I* had done for them. No sir. Well, to heck with that.

In the dining room a butler was setting plates on a fine, long walnut table. He smiled at me. "Dinner will be a while yet, young master, but I think Cook might have a treat for you to tide you over."

"Very good, Jeeves," I said breezily and walked through the china cupboard. Gosh, this is a swell house, I thought.

The kitchen was full of good smells: baking bread and sizzling roasts. A line of pies stretched across the counter and I peeked eagerly to see what kinds. A hand slapped mine as I reached for a plate of cookies.

Cook stood behind me, her eyes shining with merriment. Her curly hair was tucked neatly under her chef's hat and she was just so fat and jolly I wanted to hug her.

"Now, young master, you'll spoil your dinner."

"Aww, please. I'm so hungry," I whined as if I were only seven years old.

"Well, tell you what. As long as your father doesn't find out I guess it's all right. You can take the plate, but you have to eat them down in the cellar, so your father doesn't see."

"Gosh, wouldn't want old dad to catch me sneaking treats." I nodded happily and took the plate piled high with cookies, and a tall tumbler almost as big as me filled with cold, foamy milk.

"Right through there, young master. Mind your steps in the dark."

Somewhere in the distance I heard a faint, vaguely familiar voice screaming, "Winston! No!"

I couldn't imagine for the life of me who Winston might be. Perhaps he was one of the servants, and he'd placed the silver on the wrong side. Or maybe it was one of those horrid children I'd seen playing in the parlor.

I ducked quickly through the door and stumbled down a flight of steps, my milk and cookies flying through the air around me. I landed with a thud.

I groaned as I sat up. Ahead I saw the faintest shimmering of light. I couldn't remember why I was here. I raised my arms and shifted myself against a wall to rise. I was in a long hall or tunnel. I could easily reach the walls on either side of me.

Confused, and a little frightened, I began to whimper. I fell to my hands and knees looking for cookies, but then forgot what I was looking for and just sat there breathing slowly.

Warily, I rose again and started toward the light. After a while I stepped out into a wide room. The room was dark except for a small fire in the center. A caped figure knelt in a strangely inscribed circle on the floor. Before him I could see pieces of my knapsack, my flashlight, and part of a candy bar. I became aware of other figures lurking in the gloom. I should have been more afraid, but somehow I couldn't think straight.

The figure in the circle raised its head, and I could see the light of its eyes gleaming at me.

"Arrogance. As I told you, child, arrogance is a flaw."

He waved his hands and I was immediately released from whatever spell he'd had me under, and the full weight of what I'd done, what I'd let happen, fell on me. I thought of the sword and tried to reach for it.

There was a sudden *snap* in the air, and I felt myself lurch off balance. I heard the figure cry out, "Now!"

For a moment I sensed nothing, but then I realized I had the sword, and I took comfort in that. I stood pivoting right and left waiting for one of them to try something, hoping my friends wouldn't fall into this trap.

The figure rose and gestured. "Take him away," and several people moved into the light. They moved soundlessly, and I knew by watching them that they all were ghosts. Their faces showed little emotion beyond a certain mournfulness.

I prepared myself for battle, but they walked right through me, and all my slashing in the air did nothing. I turned to attack again and that's when I saw it.

The ghosts stooped and lifted the boy into the air and carried him from the room. I was the boy they carried. My lifeless body hung limp and dead in their arms. I thought they'd passed through me because they were ghosts, but I'd been wrong.

The ghost was me!

9

I followed the shambling pallbearers of my lifeless body deeper underground. We came to an open area. The walls and floor were metal of an odd, greenish color that ran in large hammered sheets right up to a massive door.

Through the door I found myself in a large tomb or vault. Caskets were piled everywhere, and heaps of human bones spilled from dark holes in the walls. My body was placed in a stone coffin. I leaned over the side and looked down at myself, trying to see if my body breathed or not.

The ghosts that had carried me began to wisp away, like smoke in a soft wind, and before long I was alone again. I called out but heard no answer. Angrily I slashed my useless sword at the wall. It passed through the wall as if it wasn't there, and left no sign of its passing.

Somehow I'd been tricked out of my body, and I

had no way of knowing how to return, or even if such a thing were possible. Again I flailed, frustrated, at the walls, and stopped suddenly when a strange voice said, "Watch it with that thing, will ya? Criminey, ya almos' took me head off."

I watched in astonishment as a young boy stuck his head through the stone. He felt gingerly at the top of his skull, and gave me a mistrusting look.

"Who are you?" I asked.

"Now there's a fine thing, innit? How'd you feel to find a burglar in your room, and when you stopped him from killing you he says to you, 'Who are you,' like it was his own house, eh?"

Whoever he was he talked a mile a minute. His voice sounded almost musical. He stepped all the way through the wall, the stone vanishing within his body then reappearing as he stood on the floor. He stood a full head shorter than me.

"I'm sorry," I said. "You surprised me. My name is . . ."

"I know very well who ye are, ya scallywag. You think a feller wouldn't know the people in his own home?"

"But you just said a burglar . . ."

"I know what I said. That was then, this is now. Be a mighty boring man that thought the same way about every point all the time, now wouldn't it? No, the world's too small for the single-minded folk, that's what I say. Ya like a sunrise, don't you?"

"I beg your pardon? A sunrise?"

"Course you do. Everybody likes a sunrise. Wants to see one. Sleeps in anyway, eh? Eh? Two minds at once and that's a simple thing to understand, now innit? Eh? Where's your tongue, are ye daft or what? Name's Scuttle, by the way. We'd best be going."

I grinned despite myself. "Scuttle, huh? Well, pleased to meet you, young ..."

"No time for that, you fool. Be on your way." For a small kid he had the strength of a bear. He grabbed my shoulder and threw me through the wall before I could blink. I fell onto a patch of bright green grass. The sun shone bright above me, and as I sat up, I saw we were in a cheery forest glade. There was no sign of the house anywhere around.

I got to my feet slowly. I watched two small, misshapen lumps of pinkish stuff start toward me. The closer they came the more they looked like dwarfish mannequins, but without facial features or eyes. To be truthful they were kind of cute until one thumped me in my belly.

"Hey, watch it," I said and kicked it where its chin should have been. It tumbled backward, and I brandished my sword at the other. The second one squirmed and an arm-like projection reached from the lump. It shimmered and changed until a miniature replica of my sword formed. It swung at me and I barely parried in time. I attacked more forcefully, knocking it back. It fought clumsily for a moment, then retreated to the side of its mate to await developments.

"Ah, met the minkins, eh? They're everywhere, the nasty little beggars. No sense at all. Live to fight, yet I've never seen a single traveller to the astral planes lose a battle with one. Always ends the same with them posting themselves a ways over humped up and waiting for you to give up."

Scuttle moved to join me, and I gave him a more careful appraisal. Although he looked younger than me, there was a quality to him that made me think again, a kind of wisdom in his eyes that warned me whatever else he might be, he wasn't just some little kid.

"I have to get back to my body. Can you help me?" I said. It relieved me a little to know I was on an astral plane. Broccoli had once explained astral projection, what most people call out-of-body experiences. Such experiences weren't as uncommon as many people thought, and I knew there might be a chance I could return to my own world.

"Not so fast, Mr. Chronicler. You're in Scuttle's hands now, and I don't know that I'll help or not. You didn't just come here for a visit, you were kicked out of your carcass by some high-power earth magic. You don't just click your heels and say there's no place like home, ya know."

"But Broccoli and the others . . ."

"Come on. Race you to the pond," he shouted and was off like a streak.

I stood bewildered, then ran off after him. Strange as he was he was my only chance to get around for now. I didn't dare lose him.

By the time I reached the pond he was already in, jumping and splashing like a dolphin in the water.

"Gar, but you're the slowest spirit I ever saw. How you plan to beat the likes assembled at the skull I'll never know." He dove again and came up sputtering. "Lookit this! Lookit! A shell!" He ran splashing gaily from the pond and gave it to me. "Hold it to your ear and hear the ocean."

I held it to my ear and suddenly heard the screams and cries of my friends back at the Caliban House. What was happening to them?

I cried out in horror and dropped the shell.

"What's the matter? Crab in the shell?" Scuttle said, giggling.

I grabbed him by his bright red shirt with my left hand and put the sword to his throat with my right.

"You did that on purpose, you jerk. Why?"

Scuttle grinned and my hand began to burn. I looked down and the ground was awash with the little pink things all cluttered about my legs and thumping at me with their fleshy little paws.

I looked up and Scuttle was gone, replaced by two

more of the creatures groping for my eyes. I fell to the ground still grasping my useless sword. The things swarmed over me. The texture of their flesh was strangely familiar, and the scent was like luncheon meat. As I lay under them, my face nearly covered, the whole ridiculous nature of my plight took over.

Pure blind anger fueled me. I found strength where none existed, and suddenly I was on my knees slashing my enchanted sword in a deadly arc.

"I refuse!" I shouted and made it to my feet. The creatures were beginning to clear back, wary of the sword. "I refuse to be beaten by little men who smell like Spam!"

"Spam!" Scuttle suddenly bounded out of nowhere. He'd changed his clothing somewhere and now looked like a tiny cowboy. "The minkins are all over you, almost killin' you, and you fight back because they smell like Spam? That's wonderful!" He stooped and grabbed one of the Minkins and sniffed thoughtfully. "They really do smell like Spam." He took a bite, then flung the little creature away. "Taste like it, too. Hah!"

He turned back to me and his body grew. In a wink he towered over me, and I had to crane my neck to see his face.

"Now the rules. Do not molest me again. I am Scuttle and I don't mess around. You got away with it the last time because that Spam thing was interesting. Been a few hundred years since I heard anything really interesting, so I'll let the first one slide.''

I pointed at his face way up above. "You started it. You tricked me with that shell."

Suddenly he was back to normal size, if that was his normal size. "Didn't trick you. I just—showed you something."

"You tricked me and you know it. Now why did you bring me here?"

He frowned. "Bring you here? I didn't bring you here. That ghoul at the skull brought you."

"You know what I mean. To this pond. Away from the house. If I'd stayed back there maybe I'd have found a way to help them."

"Probably not. You see, you really messed up underestimating the situation. You thought you had a standard haunted house. Not so, Milo. You let them get your gear and cast a spell on you. The Key could have cast a protective spell but noooo, you guys are too experienced, and too tough to be afraid of a little ghost. You tried to show off for the big kids."

"All right, all right, don't rub it in." I sighed and looked around me.

"What's your beef, Keef? You should be happy. Birds are singing in the trees. Fluffy clouds powder puff across the sky. The air is full of Spam. What more could you want?"

"I want to get back. Can you tell me how?"

"Okay. Since you ask so nicely. All you have to do is follow that path. Three times along the road you will be tested. Every time ye pass a test, it will raise ye up to the next plane. After the third test, you will reach the plane where the Spirit Woman lives. She will help ye if she wishes."

"What if I fail a test?"

"Then something big will probably eat ye."

I sighed again. "I was afraid of that."

"Hey, you're a shoe-in. You're the Chronicler." He clapped me on the back and pushed me toward the distant path. "I'll see you when you get to the Spirit Woman."

I turned and looked back. "And how will you get there?"

He laughed again. "Hey, I'm Scuttle. All the planes are mine."

"And how did you know I was the Chronicler?"

He waved and began to shimmer in the heat rising from the ground. "I told you. I'm Scuttle. All the planes are mine. Even the one that holds your destiny." And then he vanished just like that.

Humps of curious, patient minkins spread across the forest floor to either side of my path like a little doughy army. What real choice did I have?

I followed the path into the woods.

10

I had gone a long ways down the path when I began to sense eyes following me. I stopped and looked carefully into the dim woods away from the path. Someone was watching me; I felt sure of it. But I saw no signs of anyone no matter how hard I looked.

The path was hard, and well travelled, and though I was pretty sure it would be easy to get back to, I was nervous about leaving it to search in the bushes. Anything could be hiding back in those trees. And if I lost my way I might never find my way back to my own reality.

I brandished the sword in warning, just in case the spy was watching, and hurried on. I worried that I was taking too much time. Who knew what was happening to my friend Broccoli back at that house? I resented having to spend all this time wandering with no purpose. Why couldn't Scuttle just take me to the Spirit Woman, if she was the key to getting back? Why all this lame nonsense with tests and junk?

The path began to curve, and the trees began to thin as my way grew brighter. I came to a small brook that bubbled beside the path. The water looked very clean and cold, and I realized I was very thirsty.

I stopped to bend down and take a drink. A scuffle in the bushes to my left drew my attention before I got a drink, and I turned toward the noise, suspicious.

"Who's there?" I said in what I hoped was a calm voice.

The bushes trembled and a small creature waddled from them. It looked kind of like a hedgehog, but with a smushed-in face. It stopped and sat back on its tail blinking its eyes at me. The wrinkled, smushy face of the creature looked strangely wise. I was not surprised when it began to speak.

"The brook is mine," it said.

"Is it?"

"It is, and I forbid you to drink from it."

"I see," I said, weighing this carefully. "Is there a reason why you forbid it?"

"Because the brook is mine, and I do not wish it."

"Very well," I said, wondering if this were the first test. I thought carefully. If this were the first test then obviously there was a right thing to do

65

and a wrong thing. "Suppose I just took a drink anyway?"

"Then there would be consequences. There always are when rules are broken."

While he talked my thirst grew. Suddenly, there was nothing I wanted more than a drink. I looked longingly at the stream.

"Why do you call it a rule? Is it written down somewhere? Does it say that no one can drink from this stream without your permission?"

The animal made a strange sound, like a little whistle, and it shook its quills as if resettling them.

"Anybody can drink from this stream. Except you. Because it is mine and because I do not wish it."

"And why is this stream yours?"

"Because I felled the trees that turned the river's course, and made the brook that you see here."

"And was the river yours?"

"Of course not."

"And was the tree yours?"

"Of course not."

I thought again. I dipped my hands into the stream and brought out water then put my lips to my hands and drank.

"What are you doing? I told you you could not drink from my brook."

I looked at the creature and said, "I didn't. I drank

from my hands. With my hands I diverted your stream even as you diverted the river. The brook was not yours until you changed a river's course with your trees. And so, the water was not mine until I changed its nature with my hands. So I did not drink from your brook and there should be no consequences."

I stood and looked down at the creature who sat there shaking his head.

"Was this a test?" I asked. "Did I pass?"

"It was a test and you have failed. Oh woe to your friends. Oh woe."

And with that the creature waddled back into the bushes leaving me staring after it.

Well, heck, I thought. That wasn't very fair. Sullen, I carried on down the path. After a bit I came to an open glade. A portly gentleman sat staring at a chessboard on the table before him. A small waterfall dribbled down the cliffside behind him.

"It's about time you got here," said the man. "Sit down. It's your move."

The man looked strangely familiar. His hair was very thin and snow white from great age. It came to a V on his forehead. His cheeks were swelled and the veins in them shone through his pale skin.

I studied the board for a moment and then said, "Where is black's king?"

The man waved a hand. "Gone. Left the board."

It looked like all of black's pieces were attacked

by white's pieces, and vice versa. "How can black play without a king?"

"Can't," the old man said. "So the first move has to be to return the king."

"But if I use the move to return the king, white automatically wins."

"True, true."

"So what's the point?"

"Eh? Point?" The man looked at me with genuine astonishment. "The point is the game's begun. It must be played."

"Black can resign."

"Black cannot resign without his king. The king is gone and must come back."

I rose and knocked the board off the table. "This is stupid. There's no right answer to this. Is this another test?"

The man shook his head sadly. "It is and you have failed again."

"Well, I don't care. Your test is stupid and you're stupid, and I'm not doing any of it."

I stomped away further down the path. I wanted to cry I was so frustrated. Talking hedgehogs and unwinnable chess games. What a bunch of nonsense. I was on serious business.

I came to a bridge and a man stood at the edge barring my way.

"Now what?" I asked.

"I am the guardian of this bridge. If you would pass you must answer riddles three . . ."

"Oh, right. Riddles. Where do you people get these ideas?"

The man drew himself up as if his dignity were offended.

"I beg your pardon, but riddles are a well known staple of classical quests."

"Well, I could care less. I don't know any riddles. I don't want to know any riddles. And I'm not guessing any riddles."

The man looked around as if afraid someone was watching. He leaned forward and whispered. "Would you lighten up? Look, a job's a job. They put me on this bridge to ask riddles. Is that my fault? A man's got to earn a living. Now look. I'll ask you three easy ones and you can be on your way with no one the wiser."

I gritted my teeth.

"Oh, please? Three easy ones. I swear."

"All right, let's get it over with."

The man positively beamed. He straightened himself and said, "What manner of thing am I that is black and white and read all over?"

"Are you kidding?"

"Is my riddle too difficult for you?"

"A newspaper, all right."

"Truly, thou art a formidable riddler, young sage.

But can thou tell me how one ascertains that an elephant has been in thy refrigerator?''

I snorted with disgust. "Footprints in the butter. What is this?''

"And last, good sir, why . . ." Suddenly his face became sly and slightly evil. I realized I'd been set up. Shapes began to emerge from the rocks around us and there must have been a dozen armed figures closing in on us. "Why, good sir, is a raven like a writing desk, eh? Surely you know the classics. Can you tell me?''

I knew my life—whatever that meant on this plane—was in the balance. But for once, I thought maybe I had an advantage.

I grinned at my puzzler. "A raven is like a writing desk because they appear in the same riddle.''

A look of pure shock crossed the puzzler's face and a clap of thunder sounded over our heads.

A voice came from the sky and I cowered as the shambling figures closed in on me.

"Three tests, three failures! And now the price!''
The figures attacked.

11

One second I'm standing in front of a bridge surrounded by menacing figures, the next it was like I was at the bottom of a well. Bright sheets of light flashed in the distance, but gave no illumination to whatever place I stood.

I felt myself begin to move. It was the same kind of feeling you get on an escalator, only instead of moving up I moved—it's hard to describe, really—I guess you'd say I moved elsewhere.

The blackness began to change softening, gradually growing purply then almost rose colored. The air seemed choked with pleasant smells, soft pines, and flowers. There was a clean, animal smell around me, and I felt my astral being sigh almost despite itself. Whatever place I was being taken, it was a good place.

I found myself at the edge of a mountain lake. Faint scents of wood smoke carried across the breeze, and a long canoe sliced toward me across the still water. A pair of Indians stepped out of the canoe and started waving me towards them.

Despite the aura of good feeling in the air, I remained cautious as I stepped gingerly into the canoe. The men laughed as I tottered in the narrow craft, catching my balance. One gestured with his hands, pushing down on the air, and I knew he wanted me to sit. The Indians climbed in, sitting fore and aft with me between, and we began to cut like a birchbark knife through the dark water.

The Indians wore thick buckskin shirts and trousers, and their hair was heavily decorated with feathers, quills, and bits of wood. The man in front had blue spots on his face, like tattoos, but there was nothing menacing in his manner.

The woods around the lake teemed with wildlife. I saw bears and wolves and deer at different times during our long journey across the lake. Birds of prey soared majestically above, and I thought this land must be very much like America had been before the arrival of the Pilgrims.

Eventually we came to the opposite shore. Long structures of rough wood stood on stilts at the edge of the forest. A small hawk sat on a pole above a lodge house watching us. The tattooed Indian pointed to the hawk and then me, jabbering excitedly in a language I did not understand.

Something about the bird attracted me. Without thinking I held out my hand and the bird launched itself from its roost and swooped across the hundred yards or so between us, landing in a flurry of grace and power on my hand. Its talons bit into me and I could feel blood running, but there was no pain. The hawk regarded me with wise eyes, then stretched its wings to beat the air. It gave a cry that wrenched my heart.

I dipped my hand and launched the bird again, watched its beautiful flight until it became a speck in the distance.

The Indians looked at me with grave expressions, then walked up the slope toward the long houses. I followed them to the central building, where they lifted a leather latch from the door and swung it wide. I ducked my head and entered.

The air within the lodge was very warm, but not unpleasant. Odors of cooking meat and smoldering tobacco filled the air. At the far end of the lodge sat an old woman. The others motioned me forward and I crossed the lodge. Behind me the men withdrew, leaving me alone with the old woman.

She gestured for me to sit before her and I did. I noticed I still held my sword and began to wonder if I was doomed to carry it forever. I made a great show of putting it beside me on the floor. My hand should have been tired but it was not.

The woman sat wrapped in blankets and smiled down at me from her cushion of soft boughs. She was very large, her face as wide as Mom and Dad's put together. Her skin seemed smooth as polished wood, and I could not have guessed her age.

"Are you the Spirit Woman?" I asked shyly.

"I am," she said. Her voice was deep, and soft, and as she spoke I felt peaceful and happy. An aura of health and well-being radiated from the woman.

"I thought I failed the tests."

"There were no tests, young traveller. Scuttle is a trickster. He brought you straight to me by the fastest route, but he entertained himself along the way. He is like that. Remember it in the future."

"He's a liar then. Is he a demon or something? Is he evil?"

The woman sighed. "He is no demon. He is Scuttle, a being of the astral world, a force which is both of and outside reality as you know it. As for being evil . . . Is the wind evil? Is the rain? Yet there are floods and hurricanes. Like nature, he simply is, and for that we give thanks as we do for all the Great Spirit's creations."

"I see," I said.

"No, I doubt you do. Now, what would you have of me?"

"Answers," I said. "Is it too late to save my friends?"

74

"It is both too late, and too soon. You are beyond your world. Since Scuttle brought you here all time has passed and no time has passed."

I struggled to understand her. Eventually I said, "Then it's not too late to go back and help rescue them."

"No. It's not too late."

I almost wept with relief. We still had a chance. When I'd heard them screaming through the shell, I thought for sure that I had ruined everything. But that had been another of Scuttle's little jokes.

"Tell me, what is the secret of the Caliban House?" I asked.

"There is no secret to the house, but rather in what lurks beneath. Do you know the story of the crystal skulls?"

I shook my head.

"Long ago," she said, "when the Old Ones still held claim to part of your world, a great artisan fashioned four perfect crystal skulls for the people of the earth. He summoned champions from four corners of the world and gave each a skull. The champion of the land where you live was from the Mound People, the civilization that lived before my own.

"Each champion returned then with a skull to capture the spirit of an Old One and end their dominion in your realm once and for all. In your own time three of these skulls have been found, recovered, and are clear of the spirits of the Old Ones.

"But the fourth skull lies beneath the house you speak of. It was never returned to the artisan for the exorcism of the Old One, but was stolen by a shaman of the Mound People for his own purposes. He was one of those who used medicine for evil, and the Old One within the skull corrupted him further, until the shaman was totally mad.

"For centuries my people avoided the place where the shaman had retired with the skull, a place of great power. Bad luck happened to all who passed over. It was not until the coming of the white eyes that anyone tried to live there. Many houses have stood in that spot, and the skull has grown in power with each generation. For the Old One within the skull is the Soul Catcher, Yag Saggoth, and all who die within those halls are his to use forever."

I shuddered thinking about it. How many spirits had he taken over the centuries?

"What is an Old One?" I asked her.

"The Old Ones are the gods who warred against the Great Spirit. Their world lies beyond our own, beyond even these astral steppes, though within Scuttle's ability to travel."

I thought about that a minute, then asked, "What about Booker? Encarna said his spirit is still inside the house. But Booker didn't die there."

The woman nodded. "True, the Soul Catcher has grown in power. It is a great tragedy that he is capable of stealing the spirit of one not yet dead. As he has nearly stolen yours.''

I waited for her to explain further but she only watched me, waiting. Apparently, it was up to me to ask the right questions. She would volunteer nothing, it seemed, unless I asked. Finally I said, ''Can this Old One escape on his own? And if he does, what would that mean?''

''Not on his own, but with the right talisman he could return. It would mean the end of life on earth as you know it, for his coming would breach the barrier between worlds, and the other Old Ones would return as well.''

''The right talisman,'' I whispered. ''Like the Robe of the Thaumaturge.''

She inclined her head forward, eyes closed. ''Like the robe.''

I struck the floor beside me in frustration. ''Then I have to get back. I have to warn Broccoli while there's still a chance. He'll know what to do.''

The woman sighed and looked away from me. ''I'm afraid that that is impossible.''

''What? You mean I *can't return!*''

Pity crossed the woman's face, and I felt the clutch of real fear inside. I wanted to crawl into a corner and cry.

''The spell which ejected you from your body is incomplete. It is a binding spell. Should you return

77

to your body it would complete the spell, and enthrall you to the Old One in the skull.''

''Enthrall me? What does that mean?''

''It means you would become his creature. And he would send you to collect the robe. Armed with your power and the sword, you would become an awesome warrior. The Key could not resist you.''

''But, but I have to go back.''

''If you return the Old Ones will prevail and all is lost.''

''And if I don't return? How do we know the Old One won't still get what it wants?''

''We don't,'' she said.

I stood and glared at the woman. ''You're no help at all. It's no different than the chess game Scuttle set up. If the king is off the board you cannot move, but if you return the king it means you lose.''

The woman closed her eyes again. Her face remained impassive. ''I cannot change what is. I have no choice but to tell you the truth.''

I stooped and retrieved my sword. I raised it in the air and spoke. ''If I've learned anything, it's that the Key must not be thwarted. You say this Old One is some kind of big deal. Well, maybe so. Broccoli and I have faced some pretty big deals before, and we found a way to win. Life isn't like a chess game, anyway. That's what Scuttle was trying to tell me. He wasn't tricking me at all. He was showing me something. When all else fails, there's still a way to win the game.''

''Oh?'' Her eyes opened again, and I could see something fire-like in the depths of them. My insight as the Chronicler came fully forward, and I knew that this had been the real test. The only test. Fate was on our side, but it would give us no easy help. She continued to stare at me, and I could feel the force of her power in the air around me.

''Oh?'' she repeated. ''And what way would that be, young warrior? How do you win the unwinnable game?''

''The way anybody would if the stakes were high enough. You cheat.''

There was a pop in the air, and Scuttle appeared squatting in a corner of the room.

''And you thought I was just a trickster. I keep telling you, old woman. Ya just don't appreciate me.''

I smiled at Scuttle and gave the old woman a triumphant look.

''I knew I was right. I knew there had to be a way.''

''There is the barest chance, but you had to discover it yourself. I am not empowered to direct you,'' she said.

I turned to Scuttle. ''You are the master of the planes, correct?''

''I told ye I was. Repeating what I say is a stupid thing to do, innit? You need to move forward.''

"Spirit Woman, is it true the others will remain safe so long as they stay inside the parlor?"

"For a time, yes. Not forever."

"It doesn't have to be for long." I turned back to Scuttle. "Can you get them here? The four of them? Can you bring them out of their bodies and bring them here?"

"What do you think?"

I grinned. "Course you can. You're the master of the planes. All the planes. Will you bring them to us? And promise not to trick them? Will you tell them everything I've learned so that we don't waste time?"

He frowned and looked bored. "So what if I do? What's in it for me?"

"I promise you we'll all do something interesting. Like you said, it's been a while since you had anything really interesting to do, eh?"

He thought for a minute. "All right. Done. But it better be pretty interesting. Hard to get the interest of a guy as fascinating as me, innit?" He winked once at me and once at the Spirit Woman. "Back in a tic." Then he disappeared.

Before I could even sit down again he was back with the others. Broccoli ran to my side and clapped me on the shoulder.

"Man, you really had me worried," he said grinning like crazy.

"Well, don't stop worrying now."

Encarna stared at the Spirit Woman as if transfixed. Deion and Pete looked about them warily.

"All right," said Scuttle. "I did my part. Now where's this interesting thing we were going to do? And disappointing me is a bad idea, innit? Well? What's the plan?"

I gave him a crooked grin. "Scuttle, Broccoli and I need you to take us inside the skull. To the dimension of the Old Ones." His eyes widened and his jaw dropped. I noticed his color went a little pale. "Something wrong?" I asked.

He shuffled his feet. "Well, heck, it didn't have to be *that* interesting."

I laughed as Encarna ran to the old woman and embraced her. "Grandmother," she said.

12

"**G**randmother?" I said, surprised.

"Forget her," said Deion, spinning me to face him. "Where do you get off bringing us out here? Who do you think you are?"

I grimaced. "It doesn't matter who I think I am. I couldn't just leave you at the mercy of the skull. At least while you are here your spirits are safe. Would you rather be taken like Booker was?"

"We can take care of ourselves," he said, his jaw jutting forward. He clenched his fist in anger, and I could tell he wanted to swat me one.

"Maybe so. But it seemed like the right thing to do. I can't go without Broccoli. I need him to help defeat the Old One. Scuttle explained all that to you, didn't he?"

"He did," said Pete, stepping forward. He put a restraining hand on Deion's arm. "But what makes you think you'll win? Suppose you lose and our spirits are stuck here?"

I shrugged. "There are worse places to be stuck. And if the Spirit Woman is right, *our* reality won't be a great place to live in anyway. Because if the spirit behind the skull defeats us he'll get the robe, and once he has that power, it's pretty much all over."

"So we're just supposed to sit here on our hands while you two go off and make like heroes?" Deion shook his head. "Forget it. Like it or not I'm going with you."

Encarna's voice made us turn to her. "We're all going," she said. I gasped at the sight of her. She was dressed like the old woman now, her long dark hair braided and strung with beads. Soft light glowed around her.

Behind her the old woman stood, towering like a mountain behind her great-granddaughter.

She said, "Behold, she who is called the Vision Child, Spirit Healer, Medicine Queen, whose secret name is Looks Far Woman. Speak child. Tell them what you see."

Encarna stepped forward and her radiance moved with her. She stopped and put her hands on Broccoli's shoulders.

"You are the Key, and your totem is the pigeon hawk. You are servant and mentor to the New King, and we of the New Tribe will follow you until his coming."

She turned to Deion and put her hands on him. He straightened beneath her touch and his stern face grew gentle as she gazed at him.

"You are the First Warrior of the New Tribe, and your totem is the bear. From this day your destiny is not your own. You must heed the Key when he calls."

A puzzled look crossed his face as she turned to Pete who watched her in open mouthed wonder.

"You are the First Artisan of the New Tribe, and your totem is the wasp. From this day your destiny is not your own. You must heed the Key when he calls."

She turned to me and a flicker of amusement flashed in her eyes.

"You are the Chronicler." And she said no more.

I stopped her as she turned away. "Don't I have a totem?" I asked.

"No." She walked back to the Spirit Woman who embraced her.

"Free them, child," she whispered, then released her.

She sat back down and looked at Scuttle who was playing jacks in the corner of the lodge.

"Well?" she said.

"About time, innit?" he said. He rose and walked over to the Spirit Woman. "It wasn't supposed to happen this way, was it?"

She sighed deeply and looked up at him. "Prophecy is an imperfect thing, at best, Scuttle. Evil has adapted to thwart the forging of the Key. Why else would the skull choose now to assert itself? But so, too, has the Great Spirit adapted. After all. All things are his creation, even evil. What is done is done." Scuttle turned to us. "Well? Are you ready?" I looked at Deion and Pete. "Are you?" Deion said, "I already said I'm going." "Count me in," said Pete. "I guess we're ready then," I said to Scuttle. "What do we do now?" "Try not to die," he said somberly. He waved his hand and everything shifted.

We stood suddenly on a shelf of rock. The air around us was crimson, and filled with moving shapes. Scuttle crouched warily before us, his head shifting back and forth. He straightened, apparently satisfied we were in no immediate danger.

"Where are we?" asked Pete.

"It's where ye wanted to go, innit? We're inside the skull."

"There are steps here," said Broccoli. He began to descend, and we followed with me bringing up the rear. At the bottom we found ourselves in a kind of blasted canyon. Strange, unearthly plants struggled from the red soil, and gently sloping walls ran to right and left.

"I guess this is the way, huh?" said Deion. Gingerly, we made our way down the strange canyon. The ground was warm beneath our feet. An odor like burning wool singed my nose, and I made a face.

"Pyew," said Pete.

Eventually the terrain began to change and the walls grew closer, the ground more rocky. A dark, red pool gleamed dully off to our right.

"What is that?" asked Pete.

"Blood," said Broccoli.

The pool began to churn and bubble. Bursts of foul gas popped from the slurpy liquid, and the Hag we'd last seen at the house began to form.

A hideous shriek came from her liquid throat as she reached into our midst and grabbed Deion, dragged him toward the swirling pool.

"Fools! Would you take us in our place of power? Now you will all die!"

Broccoli grabbed at her as he had at the house, but this time she merely shrugged him away, as her bony arm closed around Deion's throat.

"The robe can't hurt me here. The master will have it soon, and all will be ours."

She was almost completely solid now, her face cracked and ancient. Her hair writhed like worms atop her misshapen head. Her nose bristled with black hairs, and her lips hung slack and slimed with drool.

She shifted Deion in her grip and held him before her.

"And now my ebony pretty one, a kiss from your old crone."

Beside me, Scuttle hissed, "Succubus!" between his teeth.

I swung my sword at her, but she dodged, and I nearly struck Deion instead. Pete leaped into the pool and grabbed her around her waist. He hung on like a terrier as she cackled madly.

Encarna suddenly grabbed Broccoli by the hand, then put her own hand on Deion's shoulder. The Hag stopped moving, and they stood there together like statues.

"Go ahead," breathed Encarna. "Try it. Try to steal his soul, and know that with it comes mine and his as well."

Anger further distorted the Hag's face, and she cried out in frustration. "He's mine, I tell you. Mine."

I saw my chance. I stabbed her in the side beneath her arm. She began to shriek uncontrollably and Deion and the others were all thrown free like rag dolls as she twisted madly at the end of my blade.

Sparks flew from her, and her bony form jerked madly as if my sword were electric. It was all I could do to hold on with both hands. Suddenly there was an explosion, and she burst in thousands of ethereal fragments, showering us with the foul essence of her being.

Then she was gone, as if she had never been. I sank to the ground, exhausted.

I felt a hand on my shoulder, and looked up to see Deion nod. "Thanks, Homes. I won't forget."

"It took all of us," I said, shaking my head. I looked at Scuttle who was standing off to the side shuffling his feet nervously. "What did you say she was? A succubus?"

He nodded as Broccoli said, "It's a kind of spirit creature. They steal the souls of others with a kiss. They are akin to demons, in a way."

"That's why Encarna's threat worked. With all of you hooked together like that, it would have been too much for her."

"Something like that," she said mysteriously. "Come, we can't afford to give him more time."

"Who?" asked Pete.

"The Old One," said Scuttle quietly. "Look."

He pointed to a distant ridge above which rose a thick, ugly light that flared in tendrils like whipping snakes. It filled the sky with sick color, and I felt my soul quail before it.

"Is that—is that the Old One?" asked Deion.

"That's just his aura," said Scuttle. He coughed. "Look, this is way more interestin' than I need, innit? You guys are on your own."

With that he vanished.

"Great," said Pete. "Now we're really stuck."

A howl filled the world around us, a scream like nothing we had ever heard. The lights in the sky grew brighter, intensified even as the howl grew louder until at last we all groaned, covering our ears in pain and falling to the red ground around us.

13

After the noise died down we trudged on. None of us were feeling particularly chipper about things. If just the sound of an Old One moaning could drive us to the ground, how were we supposed to fight the thing? I struggled up the crumbly slope behind Deion. From time to time he looked back at me. His face was set in hard lines, and I knew he was thinking much the same as I. What chance did we have?

At the top the ground leveled off again. Shapes were moving around in the distance. I watched as they neared, and was surprised to see a group of minkins come wandering up.

There were six of them. They stumbled and tumbled across the red ground like lumpen clowns. I whipped out my sword, prepared for their attack, but they ignored me. All of them huddled quivering around Pete. Excited, piping noises came from the strange creatures as they clamored around him, seeking his attention.

"What are they?" asked Encarna.

"Minkins," I said. "I ran into some before. They like to fight, but they aren't very good at it, evidently. You have to watch it, though. They can change themselves into almost anything."

Pete sank to his knees in the midst of them. Their pinkish bodies trembled eagerly as he touched them one by one.

"They're so happy I've come," he said. He looked back at us. "Can you believe what they're saying?"

Encarna frowned. "Saying? We don't hear them saying anything. They sound like a bunch of cheeping birds to me."

"Oh no," he said. His face almost shone with joy and surprise. "They talk. I can't believe you can't hear them. They think I'm some kind of hero for them. They want me to—"

He stopped, his head tilted to one side as if considering something peculiar.

He reached out and grabbed one of the minkins gently, held it before him like a doll. Its body shook and began to glow. Slowly the shape changed, thinning, stretching longer and longer until at last it was like a spear. The spearhead shone dully in the crimson light, its edges glinting with promised sharpness. The other end was thickened and hard, like a club. Tentatively Pete offered the spear to Deion.

"It is for you," he said.

Deion took the spear and hefted it thoughtfully. Then he stepped back as he spun the spear like a propeller. The long shaft danced in his hands, and I knew the wonder that he must feel as I remembered my own first experience with my sword.

He stopped suddenly in a fighting stance, the spear held standing as he did, with its butt to the ground. He shoved it forward, a huge grin on his face.

"This thing is fantastic. It's like a part of me."

"As it is," said Pete. "These arms are ours forever, created to match our souls. Like—like Winston's sword, they will always be here for us when we need them. They are our match." Pete had taken another minkin and it, too, molded in his hands. "Here," he said to Deion, "this too is yours."

He gave Deion a kind of glove that fit all along the length of his left forearm. Deion looked at it curiously then flexed his fist. Four metal claws shot forward when he closed his hand. He made several swipes in the air.

"Good," he said. "Maybe this thing will still beat us, but at least I know I'll get my licks in. Any more?"

Pete shook his head. "Not for you," he said as the third minkin twisted in his knowing hands. "A shield," he said, handing the finished artifact to Broccoli. "This is proof against all weapons. Use it well."

Broccoli took the shield solemnly and fit it to his arm as if he'd worn one all his life.

A fourth minkin curled and changed in Pete's hands, until it changed into a rod about two feet long.

He handed it to Encarna. "I'm sorry, I don't know what this is for."

She nodded as she took it. The rod began to glow in her hands, and she smiled in understanding. "It is the soul wand," she said. "With this I can create the cleansing fire."

"Whatever you say," Pete said, busy with the last two minkins. Each became a glove-like affair which Pete strapped to his own arms. He sighted a fist at a nearby rock and squeezed. Darts flew from his wrist to strike, pinging against the rock.

He grinned at us. "Guess that about does it. Sorry, Winston, there was nothing for you."

"Don't sweat it," I said. "I'm already armed." I looked around at the others. The addition of these weapons had improved their spirits immeasurably. I began to think we might just have a chance. I asked Broccoli, "What do you think?"

"Obviously something is still working on our side. That means we've got a chance. It's not hopeless. So let's get going before we lose our nerve."

"You got it," said Pete.

We marched on toward the distant horizon. The aura of the Old One had vanished. Billowing clouds of dust curled above the ground ahead. We had no choice but to walk on.

At the edge of the cloud we could vaguely make out a structure within. We walked through the wall of dust and suddenly everything turned grey. Within the cloud there was very little movement of air. Thick fog curled along the ground like a living blanket. The house ahead rose stricken from the plain like a sore that had burst from the flesh of ground around it.

A black pond stretched to our right in front of the mansion. Twisted trees ran to both directions, their withered, whitened bodies like writhing witches in the gloom. Windows stared down at us like crystal eyes, and I felt myself shiver. Clumps of fungus grew in broken fingers on the bleak walls.

Pete grabbed my shoulder and said, "It's the House of Usher. The one from Poe's story. It's just as he described it."

The wide doors in the front of the house opened. Shambling, tortured figures emerged, lurching toward us. An army of the dead. Their eyes were vacant, shimmering holes in lifeless faces. Their pale flesh shone in the gloom. Deion, Pete, and I rushed forward to protect the others.

In our own reality they were ghosts, with no form to harm us, but here in the Old One's dimension they

94

were flesh and real. In moments they were upon us. We hacked and fought, but there were too many, and our weapons were of little use for these were the truly dead, beyond our pitiful weapons.

With a scream of anger Deion fell beneath a pile of them, and then I felt my own legs give as they piled on me. I struggled to escape, but couldn't move. I felt skeletal fingers at my throat. My arms were pinned to the ground. My breath came in gasps, then not at all.

Suddenly a blue wave seemed to sweep over us as I was lost beneath a heap of ghosts.

14

The ghost beings stirred, moving off and away from me. I looked with relief at Pete and Deion who were likewise scrambling away free and unhurt.

Chanting singsong filled the air, and a blue electric fire shimmered across the broken ground, ran up the trunks of trees and danced across the pond.

In the middle of all stood Encarna, her arms lifted high, the sweet, tender chant pouring from her lips. The blue fire came from her wand and from her inner being. The ghost things watched her with haunted eyes, and something else I could only just recognize: hope.

Broccoli walked forward into the midst of the fire. In the eerie blue light I saw the glimmering edges of something almost invisible wrapped about him. It rustled faintly as he moved, appearing and vanishing with the flickering light. Somehow the Robe of the Thaumaturge was being energized or made real from Encarna's flame.

The singing continued and Broccoli held out his hands to the ghost creatures. "Go to her. She will make you free. Let her free your spirits to their rest. The horrors of the skull are over for you. Go to her."

One by one the creatures walked forward reaching timidly for the Indian girl in the blue fire. The song never stopped as she put her hands to the face of the first ghost. A sweet wind blew through the air, and I found myself blinking with astonishment as the creature shuddered, then wisped away with a huge sigh. It changed to a filmy white curl of cloud in her fingers, then soared above her to vanish in the sky above.

There were dozens of the creatures, yet there was power and release for all. Deion and I gave each other wacky grins that threatened to break our faces apart. How can I explain the pure joy we felt watching these beings attain their final rest? Whatever else happened, it was worth it for this.

At last the final creature had gone and we were alone. Slowly the blue fire began to recede, and again I thought I could almost see the robe shimmer about Broccoli's form. Was it somehow linked to the blue fire?

The fire returned as it had come, to Encarna, and at last things were as they'd been when we arrived. The house loomed behind, awaiting our next move.

"Well, guys, what do you think?" asked Pete.

"So far, we seem to be doing okay," said Deion. "But I don't understand why no one put up a fight when she started freeing the spirits. I thought the Old One took his power from them."

I cleared my throat and the others looked at me. "Well, the fact is, the Old One probably figures it doesn't need them anymore. After all, it has more power at hand. It has us."

Broccoli's eyes flashed as he said, "Then maybe he got more power than he bargained for. Look, you guys, I don't know why we were all thrown together like this, but it was obviously for a reason. Somehow you three are fated to share our destiny, and we to share yours. Before I met Winston here, I knew all about him. But you three are a complete surprise. And you all seem possessed of hidden talents. I can't believe we found each other just to lose to some refugee from a bad movie."

"I'm with him," said Deion. "I'm tired of getting kicked around and led by the nose through alternate realities and every other weird thing. I say let's get in there, and find this thing—this—whatever it is, and chop it into little pieces."

"No," said Encarna. "If you do that, you'll be destroyed for sure. We must keep our heads. If Broccoli is right, if we are *meant* to be here, then there has to be a way to win. Mindless battle isn't the answer. In this plane of existence the Old One rules supreme. We cannot underestimate it."

"None of this is getting us inside," said Pete. "Are we going or not?"

"We're going," said Broccoli.

We followed the path around the pond to the front doors which were still open. Warily, we stepped through and into a great hall. A staircase ran to the upper floors folding back upon itself near the next flight. The floor was of stone, like the walls, and our footsteps made eerie echoes down the halls.

A figure stepped through a doorway, a woman dressed in white. Her dark hair hung like shadow across her shoulders, black contrast to her pale, almost translucent skin. She nodded to us, and motioned for us to follow.

The woman led us to a library, a large room with shelves running from floor to ceiling. A fire burned in a stone hearth and the caped figure we'd met before sat in an overstuffed chair, his body swallowed by his cape, his face hidden by the shadows.

"Thank you, Madeline," the figure said. His head turned to us but we could see nothing but his feral eyes. "You must excuse her. She is an indifferent hostess at best, but then, what can one expect of the doomed?"

"Is she the Madeline from Poe's story?" asked Pete.

"The very one. Sister to poor Roderick. Alas, once Roderick learned of the deal she made with the Master, he went quite mad. I won't tell you the details. Suffice it to say, she acquired a—shall we say, a unique dietary requirement? Roderick tried to kill her, poor sod, but he failed. Then he ran away. Vanished never to be seen again. Shame really."

"Who are you?" asked Broccoli.

"What difference can a name make? I have had many names over the centuries. Before the Europeans came, I was here. Before the People you so stupidly call Indians came, I was here."

"Are you the Old One?" asked Deion, and the figure laughed heartily.

"Forgive me," he said, wiping at his face as he chuckled. "Really, that is just too rich. Why, my boy, I'm going to see that you get to meet him just for that."

"Maybe we'll kill you first and then just go find him ourselves," Deion snarled.

"Oh, I don't think so. I truly don't." Suddenly the figure's voice changed, and an exact replica of Deion's voice came from the figure. " 'I'm tired of getting kicked around and led by the nose through alternate realities and every other weird thing. I say let's get in there, and find this thing—this—whatever it is, and chop it into little pieces.' " The voice changed back. A harsher tone took over.

"You are such pathetic creatures. My Master has been ahead of you every step of the way. He knows

100

every sound you've made, every word you've spoken, every thought in your pointy little heads. And now it is the final game. Now it is your turn to die."

Deion smirked and looked at Pete. "Can you believe this clown?" He looked back at the seated figure. "Here, hold this," he said and threw the spear as hard as he could into the chest of the man.

The figure jerked backward at the impact. It jerked forward. The spear had gone all the way through and protruded from his back.

"Good arm," it said and stood. "But you'll have to do better than that." With both hands it pulled the spear from its chest. Black liquid bubbled from the hole the spear made, then the hole began to close. "A lot better."

It stepped into the light, and I heard Encarna gasp. "Booker?"

"See someone you know?" it said. Then it lifted its arm, grinned wickedly at Deion. "Catch, hot shot."

The spear flew straight for Deion's chest.

15

Broccoli leaped in front of Deion, taking the spear straight on his shield. The force of the Booker-thing's throw knocked both of them to the ground.

It laughed at them sprawled on the floor.

"Booker? Is it really you?"

It looked at Encarna. "It's partly me, I guess. I've merged, and I've got to tell you, it's great. Besides, it's your fault. You knew the stories about that house had truth to them. You knew. And you sent me in there anyway."

"I didn't know it would end like this," she said sobbing.

"Oh spare me. You always hated me, all of you. You wanted me hurt. But now I'm the one doing the hurting. This form it—it loves me."

Things flashed across his face, other faces flashing in and out, and I wondered how many creatures lived inside this being. How many others like Booker had been sucked of their spirit to keep this creature alive and moving?

"And the Master—Oh, the Master has shared so much with me. So much. He has made me his own. Look!"

He ripped away the cape and Encarna screamed. His body was ringed with tentacles that waved and danced in the firelight. Instead of legs he slithered on a bulbous mound of twitching muscle.

The voice pitched higher and higher as he slithered toward us. "He makes me beautiful like he is. Soon, we'll be together, and I will be like the Old Ones. And the world will run red with your blood!"

A tentacle shot forward and grabbed me by my sword wrist. I was amazed by the power in that form. It jerked me off my feet like I was nothing. Encarna fled the creature, cowered against the wall. Deion and Pete fought like demons against it, but always the tentacles kept them at bay. I felt other parts of the creature reaching for me. Broccoli stood transfixed, and in the fire's light I thought I saw the robe again swirling about him.

Somehow, Broccoli had to save us. Our weapons were useless against this monster. If only he could somehow gain access to the Robe's power. Then I realized what I was seeing. The Robe was trying to teach me something, and I knew what it was.

"Encarna," I yelled. "Free him. Free Broccoli's

103

spirit!'' Tentacles snapped around my throat and I could say no more. Encarna looked at Broccoli confused, but I could see he understood. He ran to her, and she let him help her up.

"Do it, fast. There's no time."

Terrified and trembling, she could barely stand. But she managed to close her eyes and begin the singing. Beneath us I could feel the house shaking. The Old One was coming. I desperately tried to remain conscious, and kicked and poked at the thing holding me.

Its face had changed again, and now looked like a molten, falling sluice of flesh, with only the barest traces of humanity. Despite its power Pete's darts and Deion's spear were having an effect. I managed to get my sword with my free hand and sliced the tentacle choking me. I fell back in relief as cool air rasped down my bruised throat. I tried to speak but could not.

Encarna and Broccoli had disappeared in a ball of blue flame. The creature fought on against Pete and Deion. His arm managed to knock Pete sideways to the wall, and he fell stunned. I tried to rise, but I was too weak to move. The creature turned all its fury on Deion.

But Deion was berserk with rage. A bloodcurdling cry came from his throat. The spear and his claws were blurs in the air.

Time after time he slashed at the creature. The more they fought the stronger Deion seemed to become. Suddenly the figure was backing away, inch by inch before Deion's attack. The face changed again, back to Booker's, and he began to plead.

"Stop it. Deion. Stop it, you're hurting me. Please. I never asked to be here. Please."

"Shut up, you hose head," Deion shouted. "You aren't Booker! Now die, you jerk, die."

A final thrust of the spear into the creature's chest, a clean swipe of the claws and the monster fell, screaming.

"No! It isn't possible. I can't die. Master, you promised. Master save me!"

And the far side of the room erupted in a shower of stones and wood. The Booker-thing gurgled as the Old One rose through the floor. It smelled of earth, and dust. Its head was as wide as a station wagon. Huge, liquid eyes surveyed the room. Its mouth was a gaping maw around which tendrils snapped and waved, each ending with tiny teeth and hooks.

Deion drew back in shock. Pete came to me and helped me up.

"We have got to haul it, buddy. We don't have a prayer against that thing."

"Master, you came," said the Booker-thing. A tongue slid from the monster's maw and grabbed the Booker-thing. In a flash it drew the screaming creature into its mouth. The crunching noises that came then made me sick to my stomach.

"It's eating him," said Deion.

"So much for the hired help," I said.

Blue fire reached out from behind me and enveloped the Old One. It roared its displeasure, and I thought my ears would surely burst from the sound.

A woman's voice whispered, "Booker." Somehow that whisper drowned out the Old One's cry, and I saw a thin tendril of something similar to what had come from the ghosts outside. It wafted across the room and I turned to see it go to a woman who stood burning in the spirit flame. She was ancient, but even through her age shone an incredible beauty.

Beside her stood a man in a flowing green robe. He too seemed older than time, with long white hair and a beard that nearly reached his waist. He was the man from the chess game, and now I knew why he seemed familiar. He was Broccoli transformed.

He spoke. "Behold, eater of evil. Behold Old One, who is called Wyrm and Yag Saggoth. He is the harbinger of the last days. His coming will bring the next great war. But your time is not yet, Wyrm. The Key must not be thwarted."

His hands raised and brilliant lines of violet energy blazed dead into the face of the Old One. A harsh scream pierced the air, and suddenly it seemed as if the Old One was going to shoot into the room all at once. Instead its long, wormy form just rose higher, higher, until it broke through the ceiling and then the roof. Still it kept coming, its whole being ringed with the purple lines of force from Broccoli's fingers.

It seemed to take forever. Surely the monster must have been a thousand yards long. Then as suddenly as it had come, it was gone. We walked to the great hole it had made and looked down.

"How is that possible?" said Deion.

"Come. We have little time. He is not banished, nor is he vanquished."

We turned and followed the old man and woman from the room. The pair seemed not to walk at all, but to float over the floor. Whatever it was Broccoli was to become, it was both greater and more terrible than I had ever imagined.

In the entry hall we found the collapsed body of Madeline. Broccoli and Encarna paid it no attention. But blue flame licked out from Encarna's form and touched her, and another soul-wisp floated from Madeline to vanish above us.

Outside we gathered by the pond.

Broccoli and Encarna stood concentrating, and the rest of us could do little but watch. Their bodies shimmered and flashed with light. Once it cleared they were returned to their normal forms.

I looked around nervously. Broccoli sighed and shook his head. "It's no use. We are too unformed. We couldn't even maintain our other forms. And the robe is not enough to take us where we need to go."

"Where is that, exactly?" asked Pete.

"We have to return to our own plane. We must find the crystal skull wherever it is hidden in the house and we must do it before the Old One regroups. Otherwise we'll be back in the fire again. The skull concentrates his energy. It can be defused, but we have to find it first."

"But first we have to get back," finished Encarna. "And unfortunately, we do not know how."

"Well, I do," I said. I walked a little ways away and shouted, "Scuttle, get your treacherous butt back here. Now!"

He popped onto the ground beside me. "That's a heck of a way to talk to a benefactor, now innit? Hurts my feelings. Now I don't know that I want to take you back or not."

"We could always stand here until the Old One returns."

He screwed his mouth up and nodded. "Pretty dumb idea, innit? Well, come on. First them, then you."

"Why can't we all go together?" said Deion.

"Different locales innit? His body's way away from yours. Assuming the rats ain't ate him." He winked at me. "Be right back." They all joined hands and vanished.

I was alone beside the black pond before the House of Usher.

108

You want a thrill? Try standing in another dimension by yourself while you wait for a monster to come back. I didn't get really scared for about five seconds. Then my imagination started working overtime. I don't know how long it was before Scuttle returned but it seemed like hours.

"Miss me?" he asked.

"You ain't just a woofin'. Let's get out of this place."

"My pleasure. Follow me."

We took about three steps and I found myself back in the basement looking down at my body in the stone coffin.

"Looks okay," said Scuttle.

"What am I supposed to do?" I asked. My sword had vanished with my return to my own plane.

"Just kind of lie down in it. Should be a pretty good fit. It's your body, after all, innit?"

"Is it safe? I won't be trapped back inside the skull will I?"

"You guys did away with the Spellcaster. That puts the kibosh on that magic."

"Listen. Thanks a lot. I don't know what we'd have done without you."

"Aww." He kicked his little foot in the dirt. "Just be more careful in the future. Kind of dumb expecting me to squire around a bunch of heroes all the time, now innit?"

I grinned. "I guess so. Bye, Scuttle." I stepped into the coffin and sat down on myself. Scuttle gave me an encouraging nod, and I lay back and closed my eyes.

"Nothing's happening," I said and sat up. Only something had. I was back in my body, and Scuttle was gone.

But I was not alone!

16

"Who's there?" I asked in a shaky voice. Were we too late? Had the Old One somehow already returned with a new army of the dead? The figure stepped forward, and gestured for me to follow. It was the pale young ghost that had shown us where to find the manuscript.

I climbed from the coffin and stepped toward him. "Roderick?" The ghost nodded and moved away. It stopped again in the doorway and waved at me to come. I followed.

We moved down a long, dark tunnel. The tunnel walls were wet, and luminous mosses grew along their sides. After a while I could see nothing but Roderick's shimmering form. He stopped suddenly and pointed to my left. I turned but ran face first into the wall.

Roderick mimed a person tapping the wall. I tapped but he shook his head and pointed to a different spot. I tapped there, and a low grinding noise filled the hall. The wall parted, and a soft, brown light seeped through its opening.

Roderick entered and I followed him down a long flight of stone-cut steps. The warm light was barely enough to see by. Yet I could make out paintings along the wall as we descended.

We came at last into an enormous cavern. I shuddered as I realized that in the other plane, this was where the Old One had lain, waiting for our battle. In the center of the cavern a stone altar stood, and in the center of the altar lay the crystal skull.

Nervous, I reached for the skull, then drew back. How powerful was it? Could it hurt me just by handling it? I looked at Roderick who merely watched me, waiting. The cavern was strewn with bone and odd tools, shards of pottery, and such. As I looked I felt a slight trembling under my feet.

I looked up worriedly at Roderick who nodded frantically, then spread his arms to show that soon this whole place was going up.

I grabbed the skull and made for the stairs. Roderick raced ahead of me up the steps, then vanished at the top of the stairs.

"Wait," I yelled. "Encarna can help you. Don't go." But he had disappeared.

I ran as fast as I dared down the dark tunnel to the crypt room. The skull was heavier than it looked, and I worried I might drop it.

I retraced the way I had come and found the steps leading up to the secret door in the cellar. From this side the door was obvious and in another minute I had made it to the kitchen.

The house was completely empty now. It looked as it had when Broccoli and I first arrived. I heard the others shouting, and I hollered back just as the house gave a mighty shake.

I found them in the dining room. "We gotta run. This place is coming down."

"We have to find the skull," said Broccoli.

"Been there, done that. Now let's move it!"

We grabbed our gear from the parlor and went tumbling out the door and across the porch. It was still night.

"Geez, how long have we been gone?" asked Pete.

"Who cares, man, we're back. And I ain't never doin' that again," said Deion.

The house collapsed just as we reached the foot of the hill. It went so fast it was hard to believe it had ever been there. The caverns beneath simply opened up and took it.

I handed Broccoli the skull. It was perfectly formed, and how some artist had ever fashioned it in the first place was beyond me. A dull, ugly light glowed faintly within it.

Deion asked, "Do you know what to do?"

Broccoli nodded. "I think so." He sat on the

ground and placed the skull before him. He looked up. "Encarna?" She sat across from him.

Closing her eyes she reached out her hands. Broccoli waited until her spirit wand formed in the air between her palms. Her concentration was intense.

Broccoli spoke. "And there were four skulls used to imprison the spirits of the Old Ones, and all were exorcised save one. The People who lived with the Great Spirit were to drive away the last of the Old Ones, but their champion was deceived by the power of the ancient evil. Now this descendant of the People has come for you at last, snake. You cannot stand before the power of the Great Spirit."

A sheet of blue flame stabbed from the wand then twisted, vanishing into the heart of the skull. A violent battle of lights played inside the skull, until at last it glowed with a piercing red light that shone from the eye sockets like lasers.

Then the light was gone and the skull was empty.

Encarna's eyes opened. "It worked. The Old One is gone."

"Hallelujah," shouted Deion. The spirit wand wavered and vanished. We all sighed.

We gathered our things and started the long walk to town. In the east the first faint notes of morning were striking the horizon.

"What I don't understand, was what happened to you two. You looked so old."

114

"Winston figured it out. Let him tell it."

"The robe was the answer. It kept showing up whenever Encarna used her spirit flame. Now part of Broccoli's problem is he absorbs things like the robe but he can't use them. At least not yet. But on the astral plane we are in the spirit. We looked like ourselves because that's how we think of ourselves. But we could have looked any age we wanted.

"You see, our spirits are timeless. Scuttle gave me the clue. He's the master of all planes, including the one which holds our destiny. He even showed me once what Broccoli would one day look like, though I just thought it was a stupid chess game at the time. So I had Encarna free Broccoli's spirit, let it reach out for the alternate plane where he is mature and in control of his powers. That older, future Broccoli can use the robe, because in that spirit incarnation the Key has already been forged."

Encarna said, "And I became older when my spirit flame showed me I couldn't help him cross unless I too became my destined self. It's funny, because I remember it, yet I don't. It's like I watched myself from another room."

"Exactly," said Broccoli. "Whatever fates are guiding us let us get out of trouble, but they aren't letting us in on any secrets. I've no more idea how my other self did what he did than you do."

"You looked great, though, for an old guy. Really fierce," I said.

We came to the park, and sat on benches to await the morning sun.

"How did you find the skull, anyway?" asked Pete.

"Roderick. The same ghost who showed us where to find the manuscript. The creature claimed that Roderick had gone mad and run away. But in fact, he'd come back. He haunted the very place where his sister had been misused, unable to leave until he'd had his revenge. The Old One and his creatures never knew that all the time they were haunting the place they were being haunted as well."

"What about Booker?" asked Deion. "You think he'll be all right?"

Encarna said, "I've freed his spirit. It should return to him, and he should be back to normal."

"Great. I went out and risked my life to get a bully back in my class." Pete laughed. "I must have soup for brains."

"Maybe he'll be changed." I said.

"Are you kidding? Guys like that never change."

"But *we* have," Deion said. "Do you understand that we can never tell a soul about what has happened? Who would believe us? And yet . . . I feel good, really good about us. I feel like I belong to something important, and special."

Pete put his arm around Deion's shoulders. "You're right, big guy. We have changed. And per-

116

sonally, I kind of like it. It's like we're a part of some secret club. The Guild of the Key. Vision Child, Warrior, Artisan, Chronicler, and Key. Something like last night is going to happen to us again, isn't it?''

Broccoli gave a mysterious grin. "Oh, I expect so. In fact, I think you can count on it.''

Epilogue

Little did we know that night the things we had set in motion. Looking from where I am now, over the backs of so many years I marvel at our arrogance. Arrogant. That's what the Booker-thing had called me and that is what I was. But as we congratulated ourselves like fools, a young man twisted in his bed on the other side of town.

Booker came awake covered with sweat. He stumbled from his bed and wandered to the bathroom. He splashed water on his face, and looked at his red eyes in the mirror. He wanted to groan, but was afraid he'd wake his parents.

In the morning they would all make a fuss over him. His mother and father would call it a miracle cure. But Booker would know the real truth. He could never forget.

Once, for one brief, glorious time he had known power. Real power. And it had been good.

Now he was torn from the Master. But he could wait. There would be other days, other battles. And there must be a new gate. He had much to do. But he would do it. He would lie still, like a snake in the grass. He would plot his plots and work his will in silence, until the day came to build the gate and bring in the Great Age.

For the Master was not dead, no. He could not die. And the Old Ones had waited before. Somewhere in this town lived a great enemy to the Master. Booker must learn more about this being called the Key, and the one called the Chronicler. He could afford to take his time. The ox is slow but the earth is patient. His day would come.

In the meantime, Booker pined for his loss. He had belonged, truly belonged. No one had ever accepted him that way before. He could barely stand it. They would pay for that loss, he promised. Pay in a big way.

Booker smiled nastily and switched off the bathroom light. He lay back in his bed and let himself revel in the memories of power. The Master had not deserted him. The Master would never desert him.

And they would pay, the whole miserable lot of them.

So Booker lay in bed and dreamed his dreams of power, until at last he fell into a dreamless sleep. And at his waist, beneath his pajamas, the first tiny tentacle began to grow. . . .